A Way with Horses

Peter McPhee

James Lorimer & Company, Publishers
Toronto, 1996

James Lorimer & Company Ltd. acknowledges with thanks the support of the Canada Council and the Ontario Arts Council in the development of writing and publishing in Canada.

Cover illustration: Daniel Shelton

Canada Cataloguing in Publication Data
McPhee, Peter
    A way with horses

(Sports stories)
ISBN 1-55028-517-3 (bound)
ISBN 1-55028-516-5 (pbk.)

1. Horses - Juvenile fiction. I. Title. II. Series: Sports stories (Toronto, Ont.).

PS8575.P44W38 1996   jC813'.54   C96-930495-1
PZ7.M36Wa 1996

James Lorimer & Company Ltd., Publishers
35 Britain Street
Toronto, Ontario M5A 1R7
Printed and bound in Canada

Contents

1

Summer Days

Caroline felt the heat of the sun warm her face and the breeze toss her hair. The last bell of the school year was still ringing as she and Ian strode down the gravel driveway toward the squat yellow buses lined up along the roadside.

Caroline felt the breeze blow a little harder and could smell new grass in the fields surrounding the school grounds. Forget what the weather channel says, she thought, closing her eyes briefly and breathing it all in, summer officially arrives on the last day of school!

She shifted her scuffed and weathered leather knapsack, its weight feeling strange on her shoulder now that it was empty of the usual load of homework and notebooks.

"Race ya!" Ian said, grinning. They were walking fast, already anticipating the freedom of the next few months.

Caroline looked back at Ian, thinking her own grin must be just as wide. "You don't stand a chance, Calder!"

"Let's go then, Owen!"

They had slowed their pace a little, each keeping an eye on the other, waiting for the first leap forward. Behind them, they heard the sound of the other kids running out the front doors of the school.

"Okay! On three!" Ian said, leaning forward, ready to run. Caroline felt the muscles in her legs tense in anticipation. Even as she prepared herself for the race, she found she was smiling at her own reaction. Why did everything turn into a contest for her? And why did she love competition so much?

"One," Ian said slowly. Caroline watched his lips as they began to form the word "two" and felt herself lean a bit further forward.

"Three!" he shouted, and took off along the gravel. He had skipped saying "two" aloud. His cheap trick gave him a split-second head start, but Caroline dug the heels of her sneakers in and chased him. Everything else faded away as she concentrated on reaching the flashing red signals on the side of the school bus before Ian.

They reached the doors at almost the same moment, slamming into each other and the rubber edging of the open door. Ian, taller and lankier than Caroline, reached out for the metal at the top of the last step.

"Beat ya!" he shouted, his cheeks nearly as red as his spiky hair. For the first time, Caroline noticed that his face didn't look as freckled as usual. She noticed this, then remembered that he had just won the race.

"That's 'cause you've got longer arms! And you cheated!"

Ian was about to reply, but he was interrupted by a loud and irritating voice.

"Hey, you two!" shouted Mrs. Calhoun, the bus driver. "What do you think you're doing, slamming into my bus like that?"

"We were just racing, Mrs. Calhoun," Ian said. He was walking up the stairs now, adjusting his backpack and brushing the dust off his jeans.

"Well, you ought to be more careful. You could've been hurt, or damaged the bus!" Ian rolled his eyes and shook his head, imitating her as he passed beyond her vision. Caroline tried hard not to giggle, since Mrs. Calhoun was still looking right at her. Before she could head to the rear of the bus, Mrs. Calhoun grabbed Caroline by the sleeve of her jean jacket.

"Just look at the state you're in, Caroline Owen! Your hair is all windblown, you're all dusty and sweaty. And I saw the way you were pushing and grabbing that Calder boy. It's no way for a young lady to behave!"

"Come on, Mrs. Calhoun. We were only racing!"

"It's still no way to behave! I know you think I'm not cool or with it, or whatever the expression is these days. But some things never change."

"Yes, Mrs. Calhoun," Caroline said, trying not to burst out laughing. "You won't have to put up with our behaviour from now until September."

"You don't have to remind me!"

She let go of her sleeve, and Caroline headed to the back of the bus, where Ian was already sprawled across one of the vinyl-covered benches.

"What did she say?" Ian asked, still grinning.

"She says we think she's not 'with it,'" Caroline said, laughing.

"I think she's real groovy, man," Ian said, holding his fingers up in a peace sign.

"And she told me that I should try to behave more like a lady."

"Oh, good luck!" Ian said, laughing now. Caroline wasn't sure how to take that reaction. Then she saw Allison Gates through the window. She was walking slowly up to the bus, surrounded by her usual gang: girls who thought they were too cool and too mature, followed by a group of boys who chased them around like lost puppies. Allison held her head up as she spoke, and the breeze didn't seem to disturb her perfect hair. She was the same age as Caroline but wore more make-up than a model. Caroline decided that if acting like a lady meant acting like Allison, she'd rather stay just as she was.

"Shove over, cheater," she said as she slipped her knapsack off, using it to push Ian's legs off the seat. She edged past him to her usual seat nearest the window.

"I didn't cheat. You just hate losing!"

"Oh yeah? What happened to 'two' then?"

"I said it, kind of," he said, grinning. His grin was so goofy it made her grin as well, but she gave him a final jab in the ribs with her elbow, just to let him know she hadn't let him off the hook completely.

She watched as Allison and her group walked up the aisle, holding their books demurely in front of them. Behind them, the rest of the kids scrambled on the bus, including Jimmy Cameron, who, as usual, followed the gang of girls. Caroline looked sideways and caught Ian sneaking a glance at Allison as she walked past, while he was pretending to check the straps on his backpack. She gave him another jab in the ribs.

"What was that for?" he asked, looking a little guilty. It didn't annoy her to see the others acting like typical boys. But Ian was her best friend!

Over the noise she could still hear Mrs. Calhoun telling them all to calm down. The noise level nearly tripled as about two dozen kids scrambled to their seats. Ever since they were five years old, this same group had shared a bus twice a day. Occasionally some faces would change when a kid moved away, or a new kid moved to the area. These last few years several new kids had been added, as more and more people moved out of Calgary to ranches or acreages in the foothills. Jimmy Cameron was one of them. His family had moved to Millarville only two summers ago. It seemed that Jimmy had been around forever, though.

"You two lovebirds at it again?" Jimmy said as he fell heavily onto the bench in front of them. He threw his bag on the floor and put his feet up on the metal pole that ran from the floor to the ceiling. Even Caroline saw he was trying his best to look cool. It wasn't easy, though. Like Ian, Jimmy was all arms and legs, gangly and awkward looking. His light brown hair was dead straight and hung over his eyes. He was constantly pushing it back from his forehead.

"Knock it off, Jimmy," Caroline said, then stared out the window again. For some reason she was annoyed. She sometimes wished things could just stay the way they always were, when everyone wasn't so interested in the opposite sex. What was the big deal that she and Ian were best friends?

"And stop calling us that!" Ian added. Even he was a little touchy about people's reaction to his friendship with Caroline.

Caroline thought everyone's sudden obsession with dating and who liked who was revolting. It seemed to be the only thing that the girls in grade seven were interested in. Caroline was still perfectly happy riding her horse, Wallace, and doing all the same old stuff she had always done. Including having Ian just as a pal.

The bus had begun to move. As usual, it was the last one to leave, since Mrs. Calhoun waited to make sure that there was no traffic on the highway for at least fifty miles before venturing onto it. Ian and Jimmy began talking about a baseball game and Caroline looked out the window as the bus merged onto the highway, heading southwest toward Millarville.

On the right, looking north, she could just make out the towers of downtown Calgary glittering in the afternoon sun. Straight ahead, she saw the snow-capped peaks of the Rockies, saw the gentle, rolling landscape of the foothills gradually become steeper as the bus continued westward and home.

Caroline lay her head back against the cold metal bar on top of the bench and closed her eyes. She could hear the constant drone of the engine and the wheels on the highway, mixed with the babble of voices. It would be the last time for over two months that she would have to listen to the racket.

"So what are we up to this weekend?" Jimmy said. Caroline opened her eyes, realizing one of the droning voices was speaking to her. Caroline and Ian both shrugged.

"I hadn't thought about it," Ian said.

"We could go riding. I heard that they're opening the trails around Elbow Falls tomorrow." Every winter, certain trails and roads were closed to the public because they became too dangerous once the snow fell in the mountains.

"I want to get Wallace back in shape," Caroline said. "The GK's early this year." GK was her term for gymkhana. Usually it was held in mid-July, but because of road construction it was nearly a month early this year. It had been moved up to next weekend so that folks would be able to travel without getting held up in traffic jams. The gymkhana was a huge event and every year it drew larger and larger crowds to the Millarville Paddock. Caroline had been competing there for almost as long as she could ride.

"I wonder if Allison and her friends are going this year," Jimmy said.

"Probably," Caroline said. "With their boyfriends." Caroline knew that all the girls in her class dated older boys. Allison was dating Rob Enns, and he was in grade nine. Rob was Caroline's biggest competition in the GK. He was as good a rider as she was.

Jimmy had been sitting up straight, his back toward the window. Caroline watched him slump down, as if the air had been taken out of him.

"Sorry, Jimmy, old pal," Ian said, smirking. "Allison thinks boys her own age aren't mature enough."

"That's one thing I agree on with her," Caroline said. "Why bother with boys our age?"

"Why would any boys bother with you?" Ian said, and returned the elbow in the ribs she had given him before.

"Maybe they would if she stopped trying to be one," Jimmy said. He was grinning nervously now, as if unsure how she would react to his little joke.

"Oooh, good one!" Ian said, and gave him a high five.

Caroline decided none of them were worth talking to at the moment and turned to look out the window. She lay her cheek against the cool glass and closed her eyes for the rest of the trip home.

***

The yellow bus left behind a cloud of thick dust as Caroline walked across the road toward her driveway. Her house was a long bungalow, with a porch that stretched out over three sides. The porch with the cedar shake finish was something her father had built himself, something he was very proud of. Caroline enjoyed it, too, especially on summer evenings when they all sat there watching the sun set over the mountains. Sitting there, she could also see the stable and paddock where Wallace pranced about.

"I'm home!" she yelled out as she entered the front door, tossing her knapsack in the hall.

"We're out here!" her mother shouted from the back of the house. Caroline slapped at her jeans to get rid of the rest of the dust before walking down the hallway to the kitchen. Through the window she saw her mother and father sitting on the porch, sipping coffee and staring silently out across the rolling hills to the mountains. Caroline opened the fridge and poured herself a tall glass of ice water. She saw the remains of an early supper sitting on the counter near the sink. Only one dirty plate meant that her mother hadn't eaten yet.

Caroline sipped her water as she walked out to the porch and plunked herself beside her mother on the arm of the two-person rocking chair her father had also built years before.

Her mother slipped an arm around her shoulders and pushed back Caroline's hair with her free hand. Over the winter, Caroline had experienced several growth spurts. She was now easily as tall as her mother, with the same dark hair. It had surprised her the day she first noticed how alike they were.

"Hi, honey," her mother said. "Glad it's finally all over?"

Caroline only nodded. Everyone knew how glad she was to be free for another summer.

"Must be nice to have a whole summer off," her father said. "I should do that one year."

"You say that every spring, John," her mother replied.

"Yeah, Dad," Caroline added. "Maybe you can do it when we win the lottery."

"Maybe I'll surprise both of you one summer."

Caroline and her mother just looked at each other knowingly. Even if he could afford it, they all knew her father would go crazy if he didn't keep himself busy. He was freshly shaved and wore a clean shirt and jeans. Caroline knew that meant he would be working at his auction house tonight.

"So! What are your plans this year?" her father asked. He stood, placing his cup on the porch railing, and stretched. He was nearly six feet tall, but the brand new cotton shirt and jeans somehow made him look shorter and stockier. When he turned his head, Caroline saw some silver shine in his straw-coloured hair.

"Same as every other year. Get serious with my training."

"I was afraid of that," her father said, grinning at her.

"Enjoy it while it lasts, John," her mother said. "Pretty soon she'll have other things on her mind besides horses and gymkhanas."

Caroline sat up straight and finished her water as her parents shared a glance. She knew they thought she was still too young to understand when they spoke this way.

"If you guys are talking about boys, forget it. I think I'm allergic!"

She stood up with what she hoped was a dramatic flair and headed back to the kitchen.

"I'm going to change before I feed Wall."

"I suppose you'll be wanting some time off from your chores to train again this year!" her father called out as she walked inside.

"Only if the place can stand up without my help, Dad!"

"I guess we'll get by okay for a week," he replied.

"Thanks, Dad. You're real 'with it.' "

She was heading for her bedroom when she heard her father ask, "Did she say I'm 'with it'?"

"Kids," her mother replied, as if that said it all.

***

Wallace was waiting beside the paddock gate when Caroline arrived. He had been pacing back and forth, rubbing his nose against the higher wooden posts, as if impatient to see her.

"Hey, Wall," she cried out as she reached the fence. "Did you miss me?"

As if in answer, the gelding circled about, stiff-legged, and nickered loudly. He threw his mane around as he trotted back to the gate, waiting for Caroline to join him. Quickly, with a practised movement, Caroline was up and over the fence, standing beside her horse. Wallace pushed his nose against her shoulder, then started to rub it against the side pocket of her jean jacket. She was wearing her older jacket, the one she wore only when riding.

"Guess what?" she said softly as she rubbed the velvety hair along his cheeks. He stopped pushing at her jacket, as if wanting to hear what she had to say. He looked down at her through his long, black lashes. She saw more intelligence in those eyes than in the eyes of just about any person she had ever known.

"School's out, Wall! And I can spend all day with you now!"

Wallace nickered again and shook his head up and down, as if sharing her excitement. Then he lowered his nose again, pushing even more insistently at her pocket.

"Okay! Okay! First things first!" She reached into her jacket and pulled out the large Macintosh that she had kept there for him. Holding it flat-handed, she lifted it up to his mouth. He snatched it quickly from her hand and tilted his head back to gulp it down.

"You're welcome," she said, smiling. Wallace loved apples, but they were a special treat that she fed him only once or twice a week. More than that and he wouldn't eat his regular food. Finished, he brought his head down and started rubbing her other pocket.

"Sorry," she said, laughing, "one's all you get." She gently but firmly pushed his head away and ran her hand along his neck to his withers. His coat was usually a deep nut brown, smooth and shiny. Now it was dull and hung in clumps, the remnants of his thicker winter coat. She had been grooming him vigorously every day, and he was slowly beginning to look a little less motley.

"You're still a mess, Wall," she said as she walked around him, gently stroking his flanks, checking to make sure there were no injuries or other signs of trouble.

"I guess we both have a lot of work to do before next weekend." She had circled him completely, checking him from hoof to poll. Satisfied that he was okay, she once more rubbed his smooth cheeks.

"You still hungry?"

Again, as if he understood her words, Wallace nickered and nodded his head back and forth. He began to trot slowly toward his stall before she could even turn around. The apple was fine as an appetizer, but he was more interested in the main meal of the day. It was part of her daily work around the acreage to feed and groom Wallace. She fed him twice, once in the morning before she left for school, and once in the afternoon.

Caroline kept his stall clean and dry just inside the big shed next to the paddock. When Wallace had first arrived, just over four years before, they had converted a corner of the shed into a stable for him. Wallace had been up for sale at the auction house that her father and uncles owned. They had known that Caroline desperately wanted a pony and had seen right away that Wallace was an exceptional horse. There had been a bit of a battle back then about letting her have a horse at all. Luckily her father had won. Of course, at first Caroline had thought only about how much fun it would be to be able to ride him all the time. She had no idea how much work was involved. Feeding, cleaning, grooming and exercising Wallace was nearly a full-time job for her. What had made it all worthwhile was Wallace himself: right from the start, they had connected.

"It always amazes me to see the way that horse reacts to you." Caroline turned to see her father enter the shed. He was holding his travelling mug. Little wisps of steam escaped from the small slit on top. She was surprised to notice it, realizing it must be colder out than she thought.

She had been working up quite a sweat, grooming Wallace as he slowly munched at his supper and stopped occasionally to take a sip from the water bucket set up beside his stall. Wallace would sometimes turn to look at her as he chewed his food, as if politely listening to her speak.

"It's as if he actually listens to you babbling on like that."

"Of course he's listening to me. And I don't babble! I'm just telling him about my day!"

"And how dumb boys are around Allison Gates?"

"Dad! Don't you know it's not polite to listen to other people's conversations?"

Her father grinned and took a sip of coffee. He looked at Wallace, and Caroline knew that he was wondering if horses qualified as people. Caroline knew better, of course. There had never been any doubt in her mind that Wallace was a person.

"I just thought I'd say good night. I'll let you two finish your conversation in private."

"That's nice of you," Caroline said. She was using the heavy dandy brush to clean the dirt from Wallace's flank. She could feel her father's eyes on her as she worked the brush up and down.

"Careful not to get his legs with that," her father said, watching her closely.

"Dad! I know what I'm doing!" Caroline knew that the dandy brush's thick bristles were too coarse for a horse's more sensitive spots.

"I know you do. I'm just checking. Do you want me to check his hooves, or is that something else you can do yourself?"

Caroline could clean Wallace's hooves all by herself, but she knew that her father still felt he had to watch out for her. She had come to realize this only lately and let him help her do things she was perfectly capable of doing for herself. It seemed that there were fewer and fewer times they did things together these days. Her father came into the stall, leaving his mug on a worktable.

While Wallace continued to chew, ignoring them, her father lifted up the horse's hind legs, and Caroline used her pick to clean the muck out from under his hooves. It took only a few minutes to clean them thoroughly.

Her father made a final inspection of Wallace before dusting off his jeans and grabbing his mug again.

"Are you planning on riding tonight?"

Caroline nodded. "Ian and Jimmy are coming over after supper. We're going to set up the paddock for training."

"Do they know that?"

"Well, not exactly."

They had agreed to go riding near the end of the trip home, after Jimmy had been thoroughly convinced that Allison wasn't interested in doing anything with him. Caroline hadn't told them what kind of riding she had in mind.

"Well, make sure you give him a little time to digest his supper before strapping the cinch on."

"Dad! Don't you have to leave?" She turned to him, trying her best to look exasperated by his comments.

"Okay! I'm going now. See you in the morning." On auction nights, it wasn't unusual for him to get home well past one in the morning.

"Bye!" she said as he slowly turned toward the driveway and his dusty old pickup. He preferred it, even though they had a perfectly good van.

"It's okay, Wall," she said as she heard the door of the truck slam, and the engine roar to life. "Adults are a little strange sometimes."

Wallace nickered and shook his head slightly, turning to face her once more. She quickly finished his grooming, and loosened the halter rope so that he could walk around after he finished eating. She took one last look around his stall, then, once satisfied all was well, headed back to the house for her own supper.

***

Ian and Jimmy rode up slowly as Caroline finished cinching her saddle tightly on Wallace. He whinnied a little and shied back as he noticed the two approaching horses. When they were close enough for him to catch their scent, he settled down once more.

"So," Ian said, resting his hands on the horn of his saddle. "What first?"

"Good timing, you guys," Caroline said as she led Wallace out of the stable toward the paddock. "I was waiting for you to help setting up."

Ian just groaned and rolled his eyes. Jimmy looked at him, curious at his reaction.

"I should've known!"

"What?" Jimmy asked.

"You'll see," Ian said, dismounting. He pulled a pair of thick leather work gloves from the pockets of his jacket and slipped them on. "The usual place, I suppose?"

"You got it," Caroline said, smiling.

The usual place was an old corrugated tin shed. Caroline had scavenged the area for the last few years looking for just the right stuff to use in training Wallace. Heaped inside were old tires, poles with flags made from orange garbage bags, wooden planks used for jumps and rusted oil drums. Her favourites were the brightly painted plastic cones that she had managed to talk a construction crew out of last fall. She and Ian had carefully painted them neon orange, so that she and Wallace could easily spot them. They were wonderful for training Wallace to corner quickly in tight spots. Seeing the equipment piled up to the low ceiling, Jimmy let out a long whistle.

"Do you set this up every year?"

"She sure does," Ian said, making a face. Caroline gave him a quick shove. They both knew he was just laying it on for Jimmy's benefit. Despite all the work setting up, he knew that it was worth it for both of them. They had become better riders because of it.

"Let's get started, boys!" Caroline said dramatically, slipping on her own work gloves.

Nearly two hours later, the course was set up inside the paddock. The barrels, poles and cones made an intricate pattern that was close to the set-up used at the official gymkhana. The wooden boards made decent jumps of varying heights. The three of them mounted their horses and looked over the carefully laid out field. They were quiet now, surveying their work. The set-up had gone fairly smoothly, but had not been totally free of conflict.

"That's not where we put the barrels last year!" Ian had shouted when Caroline started to give him directions.

"So what?" she shouted back, half a dozen metres across the paddock from him. "It works better this way." Caroline had been planning the layout for weeks. While other girls in her class were scribbling notes to each other or writing their initials next to some boy's and circling them in hearts, Caroline was drawing and redrawing the best plan for setting up her paddock.

"It's dumb this way. The horses won't be able to turn quick enough!"

"Then we'll keep on training them till they can!"

"It's too narrow!" Ian replied. He and Jimmy had been holding a heavy oil drum, but Ian had let go while he was arguing with Caroline.

Seeing she was about to respond, Jimmy, his arms tired from holding the barrel alone, decided to pipe up. He let it slip through his fingers and clang hollowly on the ground.

"Would you two stop it!" he shouted. "Sometimes you argue worse than my parents!"

This had a strong effect on both Ian and Caroline. Neither one of them liked being compared to some dumb old married couple. Especially the Camerons!

"Let's just do it my way, okay?" Caroline said finally, wanting to get the last word in. "Besides, who's won more events?"

Jimmy and Ian just looked at each other, shaking their heads.

"She thinks she's really something when it comes to riding, doesn't she?" Jimmy said quietly.

"Yeah," Ian replied as they both hunkered down to pick up the barrel. "And the worst part's that she really is!"

2

An Old Indian Word

It was a time of year that Caroline loved and hated all at the same time. She loved the excitement in the air that always surrounded the gymkhana. She loved the circus atmosphere that sprang up overnight in the fields surrounding the Millarville Paddock. When she was younger, she had asked her father what the word "gymkhana" meant. "It's an old Indian word," he had said. "It means, 'mighty competition.'" She had believed him for years until she came across it in a dictionary. It was Indian all right — East Indian. It was a word the English officers adapted to name their riding events while stationed in India. As much as she loved the atmosphere, she hated the confusion and the noise of the seemingly endless parade of cars that fought each other for any available parking space.

"What a mess!" Jimmy said as they broke through the trees into a small clearing overlooking the Paddock. Caroline and Ian pulled up on either side of him and looked down as well. Jimmy was right, Caroline thought, it *was* a mess.

"I'm sure glad we decided to ride this year," Ian said patting Buck's neck. They saw cars and vans and horse trailers scattered across the fields and roads. Some were already stuck in the thick mud beside the highway. Usually Caroline was stuck down there with her parents. They had decided that this year she was old enough to go on her own. From this vantage point it looked as if a giant had come along and scattered the people and cars. She saw the stalls where the local people sold homemade crafts and foods. She could see the hot dog and cotton candy vendors and the carnival that set up kiddie rides, complete with a miniature Ferris wheel.

There were even a few bored ponies that kids sat on, held on by their mother or father, as the ponies slowly walked around in a circle. It seemed so childish to her now, but not so long ago that was her favourite part of the gymkhana. That same pony ride had been her first time on a horse.

From the hill they could smell the concessions and hear the music of the country band playing near the stalls.

"That smell's making me hungry!" Ian said, breathing deeply.

"You're always hungry," Jimmy replied. He turned to Caroline, grinning, and she saw he was waiting for her to utter one of her usual put-downs. But she had been staring off in the distance, only half listening.

The area was deep in the foothills of the Rockies and was a mixture of gentle hills and pasture that turned steeper toward the west. From the top of the hill they could see for miles, horse and cattle ranches and the huge hills covered with pine forests already turning a brighter green. The snow-covered Rockies glittered in the early morning sun.

"It's so pretty up here, isn't it?"

"I guess," Jimmy shrugged. Caroline suspected he enjoyed looking at the view, but didn't want to admit it, in case his friends thought he was weird.

"I'd rather be looking at a hot dog right now," Ian said. It was a rather pathetic joke, and the others ignored him. Caroline felt torn; she wanted to stay up here, riding in the forests with her friends, but she also wanted to be down there in the Paddock, competing. As if reading her mind, Wallace shifted his weight and shuffled forward slightly.

"Looks like Wallace wants a hot dog, too," Ian said.

Then they heard the sound of hooves crashing through the trees. Both riders and horses were startled, and Jimmy's horse, Stan, nearly tossed him as he reared up. Ian and Caroline, being more experienced riders, brought their equally startled horses under control quickly. A group of about eight kids, slightly older than Caroline and her friends, crashed through the forest into the clearing at a full gallop.

"Out of the way!" the leader shouted as he raced right at them. Jimmy was still struggling to control Stan as the newcomers rushed toward them. Caroline grabbed Stan's bridle and, kicking Wallace forward, pulled him out of the way. Ian and his horse, Buck, were almost in the trees, to keep clear of the others.

"Hey! Be careful!" Ian shouted as the riders passed them, not slowing down. The horses had kicked up a thick cloud of dust, but Caroline recognized a few of the riders. She saw that the leader was Rob Enns and that Allison Gates, looking terrified, was trying to keep up with him.

"Try and stop us!" Rob shouted back, just before disappearing over the ridge. "If you can do anything else but sit!"

Caroline saw the colour rise in Ian's cheeks. By now the others had all disappeared down the hill, and Caroline saw Ian about to dig his heels in, ready to chase them.

"I'll show him who can ride!" he called out.

"Hold it!" Caroline shouted, manoeuvring Wallace in front of him.

"We can't just let them get away with that! We can outride those guys any day!"

"Sure we can," Caroline said. "And we'll prove it in the Paddock."

"I wanna show them now!"

"Me, too!" Jimmy added.

"If we take our horses down like those guys, they'll be exhausted!"

Ian still wanted to chase them, but he saw that Caroline was right.

"Who cares if they can ride fast on a trail? Let's see how good they are in the ring!" she added.

By now the dust and the horses had settled down once more. Ian nodded his head, still wanting to race, but knowing Caroline was right.

"Okay," he said at last. "Let's get going!"

With one last glance at the mountains, Caroline and the others headed over the hill and down the trail to the Paddock.

***

Caroline felt Wallace tense under her as he anticipated the flag drop. Out of the corner of her eye, she saw Ian and Jimmy glance over at each other, and knew that they were grinning. She didn't want to take her eyes off the announcer, who was standing on a wooden platform in the centre of the arena. The announcer was Mr. Calhoun, the husband of her bus driver. He had been the announcer here since her father was her age. He was a strange-looking man, tall and thin, but with a huge round belly. She used to wonder if he hid a basketball under his shirt. His cowboy hat was antique, like the ten-gallon ones they wore in old westerns. As she deepened her concentration, the sound of the country band playing off in the distance and the pipe music from the kiddie rides faded away.

"One!" Mr. Calhoun yelled. "Two!" There was an unbearably long pause before he shouted, "Three!"

The small flag fell and the rope held up in front of the horse was dropped. Wallace was off even before Caroline dug her heels into his sides. She tensed the muscles in her legs and balanced herself over his flanks as the first barrel rushed toward them. Three barrels were set up in a triangular course in the centre of the arena. Caroline reached the first one quickly and pulled gently on Wallace's reins to make the first 180-degree turn. She almost didn't have to lead Wallace. After so many years of practice, he knew instinctively to turn at each barrel. She fell into his rhythm, letting him set the pace, moving up and down in perfect rhythm to his gait, but still maintaining control. The second barrel came up on their left, and Caroline leaned into the turn with Wallace, feeling him pick up speed as they rounded the turn and headed for the third and final barrel. They slid slightly as they turned the last one, heading for the finish line. Out of the corner of her eye, she saw the flag come down and reined in Wallace, letting him canter around the arena to settle back down. She almost smiled as she heard the roar of applause from the crowd, but she was still too tense to relax completely.

"Good boy!" she said gently to Wallace, patting his neck as they slowed to a walk. She could feel his sides heave as he got his breath back, could feel his heart beating from the excitement of the race as well as from exertion. Wallace kept his head high and almost seemed to preen in front of the crowd. It was as if he enjoyed the applause.

"That was Caroline Owen of Millarville, folks," Mr. Calhoun called out over the loudspeakers. "Let's give the little lady another hand for that fine effort!"

Caroline cringed, but kept smiling as the spectators applauded once more. She knew that Ian would love bugging her about being called a little lady.

"Come on," she whispered to Wallace. "What's taking them so long?"

His breathing back to normal now, she nudged him toward the stalls and her parents waiting there for her.

"We have the time of the last race now, ladies and gentlemen," the voice blared over the speakers. "Caroline Owen's final time was 33 seconds!" There was another roar from the crowd. Caroline felt her heart leap in her chest. She had been keeping careful track of all the other times. She knew what had happened even before the voice boomed out again.

"That beats the best score of 58 seconds, scored by Rob Enns of Bragg Creek! Caroline wins this year's Junior Barrel event!"

Caroline, still smiling, slid off Wallace as she reached her parents. Both of them were grinning madly and hugged her as she stepped up to them.

"Congratulations!" her mother yelled over the crowd. "You were wonderful out there!" Caroline knew that her mother was glad she had won and just as glad that she hadn't fallen off as she raced around the course.

"Get out there and wave to the crowd!" her dad yelled, pushing her forward, around Wallace. She had been using him as a kind of shield.

"Dad!" she whined. She didn't mind competing, but she was always embarrassed by the reaction of the spectators.

"Go on! Enjoy it! You deserve it," her mother said.

Caroline shyly stepped out from around Wallace and waved at the crowd. She saw Ian and Jimmy across from her, imitating her awkward wave. She just ignored them and turned back to be hugged once more by her parents as the applause died down.

"That makes three events that Caroline has won today, folks!" Calhoun's voice blared out again. "Not bad riding for a filly! I guess the boys better start putting a little effort in for the final event!" Caroline and her mother looked over at the judges' stand. There was a smattering of laughter at the announcer's remark.

"What a sexist!" Caroline said in disgust.

"Yeah," her mother agreed. "I'd like to see him barrel race!"

"Take a look at him, Mom," Caroline said, still staring at Mr. Calhoun, seeing the material of his cowboy shirt stretching dangerously over his belly. "We could use him as a barrel!"

Ian and Jimmy slipped under the wooden posts to join Caroline and her parents.

"Pretty good, pretty good!" Ian and Jimmy said, patting Wallace on the neck.

"Thanks," Caroline replied.

"We weren't talking to you," Ian said. "We were talking to Wallace. He did all the work. All you did was stay on!"

Caroline just made a face.

"Although you weren't too bad," Jimmy said. "For a filly and all!"

They began laughing hard at this. She felt her cheeks grow hot, even though the remarks were totally typical of the pair. Then she saw that her father was laughing, too.

"Boys!" Caroline said in disgust, and grabbed Wallace's reins. "Let's see how much laughing you do after the next race."

She pulled Wallace around, hoping he would knock her so-called friends out of the way as he followed.

"What is the next event?" her mother asked as she followed Caroline back into the stalls.

"The five-dollar event," Ian replied, looking over the crumpled program he pulled from his back pocket.

"Great!" Jimmy said. "Finally something I can compete in."

Caroline nodded. The five-dollar race was the last event, a fun ride held before the prizes were given out. Caroline thought it was a little childish, each manoeuvre called out by the announcer, like a mounted Simon-Says. She wanted to get on to the prizes.

Her mother must have sensed what she was thinking. She put her hands gently on Caroline's shoulders. "Would you just relax for once?" she asked. "We're all supposed to be having fun today, right?"

Caroline nodded and smiled. She felt a little foolish; sometimes even she saw how seriously she took things.

"You're right, Mom," Caroline said. "I should just go out and have some fun like everybody else."

"Now you're talking," her mother said.

3

The Competition Heats Up

Caroline and Ian waited side by side in the middle of a pack of twenty riders of varying ages.

"Now folks," Mr. Calhoun said. "There's been a lot of serious competition here today. Let's slow things down and have a little fun, as our contestants get in place for the final event of the day: The five-dollar race!"

There was applause and a few of the horses started, bumping into their neighbours. Rob Enns was up near the front and his horse was one of the nervous ones. Caroline and the others watched Rob struggle to get him back under control. The horse looked tired, its breathing ragged and flanks sweat-covered. Rob didn't look much better himself.

"He won't make it," Ian said softly to Caroline. "His horse is beat."

"Aren't you glad I stopped you from racing them here?"

Ian just shrugged, not willing to admit she had been right.

"For those of you not familiar with the race, let me explain," Mr. Calhoun blared out again. "All the competitors will perform a series of manoeuvres, called out by yours truly. The last one left mounted will be the winner."

Caroline and the others watched the flag, waiting for it to drop and the competition to begin. She was more relaxed in this event. There were no trophies on the line here. Like her mother had said, it was just a little fun to end the day.

"One, two...go!" Mr. Calhoun called out, and the flag dropped. "Figure eight to the left, walking!"

Some of the riders led their horse to the right, bumping into others, causing confusion on the field and a lot of laughter in the stands. Each contestant had a number pinned to the back of his or her shirt, and Mr. Calhoun began calling out the numbers of the first riders to be disqualified. They were led out of the arena to the good-natured jeers and laughter of the audience. Caroline and Ian grinned when they saw that Jimmy was one of them.

"Figure eight, right! Canter!" the announcer yelled out. The pack of riders and horses struggled to get back into formation and follow the directions. At the faster pace, even more riders stumbled and were disqualified.

The race continued and as Mr. Calhoun had warned, each move was a little tougher than the last. He called out numbers at random and the riders had to pivot, turning the horse around at a ninety-degree angle while on its hind legs. Next came a rollback, with the horse going east in a fast lope, sliding to a stop and rearing up and over to face the opposite direction, again at a fast lope. Caroline and Wallace performed both manoeuvres gracefully, and the audience applauded loudly.

After only twenty minutes or so, only four contestants were left — an older girl, Caroline, Ian and Rob Enns. To her surprise, Rob and his horse were holding out extremely well. Caroline was really enjoying herself. The competition this year was tough and Mr. Calhoun was working hard to disqualify the last contestants.

She watched Ian finish his rollback and rein back in beside her. He was hot and sweaty, and his hair stuck to his forehead under the wide brim of his straw hat.

"Not bad, Calder," Caroline said when the applause died down. "But it looked like you nearly fell off that time."

"You wish, Owen!" he said, puffing. Before they could say anything more, Mr. Calhoun's voice blared over the speakers again.

"What do you say, folks?" he shouted. "Think I've been too easy on them?" The audience screamed their approval; they wanted the competition to heat up.

"All right! Let's get those saddles off!" The audience applauded as the riders dismounted and attendants helped them remove the saddles. "You know what folks?" Mr. Calhoun said. "I still don't think this is hard enough!" Caroline remounted and shifted her weight, trying to get as comfortable as possible. All of this was just for effect since everyone knew what would happen next.

"I think I know just the thing! Attendants, please!"

To the cheering of the crowd, attendants walked back into the centre of the arena. Each of them held a five-dollar bill, waving it in the air dramatically.

"Each of the riders has to complete the rest of the obstacles without losing that bill. This isn't as easy as it sounds. We all know how hard it is to hold onto money these days."

Caroline rolled her eyes. He made the same dumb joke every year.

"Attendants, please place the bills in the appropriate spot!"

Each of the riders lifted up slightly as the attendant placed the bill under their seat on the horse's back. They left just a bit of the money exposed to flutter in the gentle breeze. Once more the audience applauded. While this ritual was happening, other attendants had been setting up the next event. Small cavallettis, jumps made up of round poles, had been placed at intervals along the arena. A crossrail jump, also made up of round poles and about eight inches high was set up at the end of the cavallettis. At the announcer's cue, each rider was to run the course separately, first at a walk, then at a trot and finally, if anyone was left, at a canter.

The older girl was chosen first. She and her horse easily made it past the obstacles at the walk. At the trot, they once more made it past all the obstacles, but at the last second, her horse balked at the crossrail. There was a spontaneous gasp from the audience as the girl lost her balance. It was only for a split-second, but it was enough for the five-dollar bill to get loose. Caroline and everyone else in the arena watched it float away before the applause started again. The girl lifted her hat and clucked at her horse. He seemed to curtsey, then they rode off, the girl waving her hat as the crowd cheered. Caroline wondered how long it had taken to teach the horse that trick.

Rob was next. "Let me show you how it's done," he said as he kicked his horse forward.

Caroline and Ian both looked at each other.

"I tell you," Ian said, "his horse is finished. He won't make it!"

"You said that ages ago and they're still going!" Caroline said. She was just as surprised as Ian that the horse and rider had any strength left. Rob, despite Ian's prediction, ran the course three times, each time a little smoother and faster. After each successful run, another five-dollar bill was placed under his seat. When he rode back to the start, he still held the money firmly in place.

Next up was Ian. Caroline watched as he rode gracefully and easily through the course. He may be a goof sometimes, she thought as he rode back to the start to the crowd's applause, but he rides beautifully.

"Well done!" Mr. Calhoun called out. "Now let's have our final contestant up. None other than our own Caroline Owen, who came in first in just about every event today. Let's see how she handles a real challenge!"

Caroline tried yet again to ignore his comments as she urged Wallace forward. Jumping was a little more difficult without a saddle and stirrups, but it was something they were both used to. Like the others, she easily made all three attempts and now sat on fifteen dollars.

"I'm getting a little worried, folks! As you know, the last one mounted takes home all that money. And it's coming out of my paycheque!"

To the obvious pleasure of the crowd, he promised to make things tougher for the competitors. Despite the corny jokes and the predictability of the event, Caroline was thoroughly enjoying herself. She saw that Ian and Rob felt the same way. This had started off as just a stunt, but the competition was getting tough. All of them felt the same rush of adrenalin and all three equally wanted to win.

More cavallettis were placed, and two more crossbars, each higher than the other, were added. The highest was now two feet from the ground. To make things tougher, an old, ragged cowhide was hung on a pole near the first cross-jump. Its movement and strange smell sometimes spooked a horse that didn't like surprises. Also, Mr. Calhoun had decided there would be no more walking. The course had to be completed at a canter.

"Here we go, Wallace," Caroline said, leaning forward to whisper in his ear. "Let's show these boys who's best!" Wallace tossed his head and pranced a little, as if letting her know that he was out to win as well. It had been a long day, and Caroline felt her arms and legs ache from all the riding. She had to ignore her aches and pains and concentrate on the course; it was the only way they could win.

Again, Rob was first up and once more he grinned at Ian and Caroline before taking off.

"I wonder what I'll buy with all that money I'm going to win!" he said just as he took off.

"How about a personality?" Ian said out of the corner of his mouth and they both laughed. Rob and his horse made it easily over the first few obstacles and headed around to the second crossbar, the one with the hide above it. Everything was going well, until, at the last moment, a gust of wind caught the hide and it flew up. Rob's horse whinnied in fright and slid to a stiff-legged halt. Rob, just as startled, lost his balance and flipped over his horse's shoulder. Caroline felt as though something had knocked the wind from her as she watched Rob turn slowly in midair. Somehow, he managed to twist himself around and land squarely on his feet, still clutching the reins. The five-dollar bills fluttered around his head and shoulders as both horse and rider tried to figure out just what had happened to them. The audience cheered his stunt.

"Wow!" Ian said over the cheers. "Did you see that move?"

Caroline nodded, her heart back in its proper spot. "He'd make a heck of a rodeo clown."

"Well," Ian said slowly as Rob was escorted off the field and an attendant scrambled to catch the flying bills, "I guess it's just you and me now."

"I guess so," Caroline replied. Ian nudged his horse forward, about to begin.

"Hey, Calder," Caroline shouted.

"Yeah, Owen?" he replied, waiting for her to insult him.

"Be careful."

He looked surprised, as if her words were not what he had expected and he didn't know how to respond. Instead of answering, he just kicked his horse into a canter. He cleared the course flawlessly, as did Caroline. It was still a dead heat. Once more the crossbars were raised, this time to over three feet. The tension in the crowd was reflected in the voice of the announcer. This was supposed to be just another fun ending to the gymkhana. No one was expecting such a display of horsemanship. Caroline could tell that Mr. Calhoun was impressed, just by the fact that he had forgotten to make his dumb jokes.

Once again, Ian and Caroline managed to complete the course, and more money was added to the pile between them and the horse's back. The music had died, and so had the sounds from the crowd. The audience leaned forward in their seats, anticipating. Caroline lifted her hat to wipe the sweat from her brow. Her thick hair was matted and had begun to work free of the tight pony-tail her mother had tied. Every muscle in her body ached; even her lungs ached with each breath. She knew that Ian was tired as well. She also knew that he was equally unwilling to give up until somebody won.

The crossbars were taken away and replaced with higher jumps, three of them, all over four feet high.

"Now kids," Mr. Calhoun said. "My insurance agent is right here." Caroline looked up to the booth and saw the announcer was still sitting all alone. "And he tells me that I have to give you the option of quitting right here and now. We'll just call it a draw and let both of you split the prize money. What do you say?"

Ian and Caroline, both hot and tired, had removed their hats to feel the cool breeze. In response, they glanced over at each other. They grinned, shoved their hats back in place and nudged their horses forward in a little circle. The crowd went wild.

"I guess we all know what that means, folks!" the announcer said over the roar. "Let's get on with it!"

Ian didn't wait for the cue; he kicked his horse forward into a lope and headed for the jumps. He cleared the first two easily, and Caroline felt pride and worry all at once. Pride because neither she nor Ian had ridden better; worry because the jumps were higher than any they had attempted before. She saw the look of concentration on Ian's face as he reined in and turned for the last jump. Caroline grabbed Wallace's coarse mane and held her breath as the horse's front legs cleared the jump. Then there was a crash, as the hind legs hit the pole, knocking it free. The horse landed clumsily, but stayed upright. Ian, clinging desperately to its neck, slid to the side. If he had been in stirrups, he would have been fine, but bareback, the movement was enough to let the money fly free.

There was a roar of disappointment from the crowd when they realized that it was finally over, then more applause. Caroline craned her neck to see if Ian was okay. Then she saw him walk around his horse, waving at the crowd, then at her.

"Well, folks. I guess it's all over!"

Caroline, still tense with the excitement of the competition, as well as worry for her friend, hadn't realized just what had happened. Ian had lost the money; she was the last one left. Somehow it felt anticlimactic. She had wanted to try the last jump, to test herself and Wallace.

As she dismounted, the crowd was still applauding, both for her and for Ian. There was a bit of a lull and she heard a faint, familiar voice over the crowd. She saw Ian walking toward her, leading his horse. He was shouting something, waving at her.

Others in the crowd heard him and began to pick it up.

"Go!" he shouted, followed by the crowd. Quickly it was picked up by more people and became a chant.

"Go! Go! Go!" they shouted. Ian was only a few feet away from her now. He was grinning and raised his hands, indicating the crowd. Caroline looked into the stalls and saw her parents standing there, watching, as stunned by what was happening as she was.

"What are you doing?" she shouted to Ian.

He still just grinned at her. "I know you, Owen. You won't be happy until you do it yourself. You don't want to win by default!"

She knew that he was right. She wanted to try the jump, to prove that she could do it. Ian cupped his hands in front of her, and she stepped into them as he helped lift her back on Wallace. The crowd cheered as the attendants grabbed all the money and slipped it back in place beneath her.

"It looks like the little lady isn't finished yet! She wants to win this for herself!" Mr. Calhoun called out.

Caroline ignored the sound of the crowd and the announcer as she and Wallace picked up speed. She saw the first jump rush toward her, and she and Wallace ignored the stiff hide flapping in the breeze. He took the jump easily. And the next. They circled back around, the crowd still chanting, "Go! Go! Go!"

Wallace fell into a lope easily and smoothly, Caroline using her knees to guide him forward. They reached the last of the cavallettis and then they were up and over the final jump. Time seemed to slow for her while Wallace was in the air, and she held her breath waiting for the sound of his hooves hitting the fence. But it never came and she felt a jolt as he landed smoothly in the soft dirt.

The crowd roared and stood. Hats and paper cups flew into the air as Caroline looked behind her. She hadn't lost a single bill. Waving at the crowd she felt her pride swell, for herself and Wallace. She leaned close to his ear and kept praising him.

They had done it! Wallace pranced, holding his head and feet high, the way he always did when he was proud of himself.

"Well, folks," the announcer said at last. "It finally happened! I'm actually speechless!"

Caroline slid off Wallace as her parents rushed from the stands into the arena. She was quickly wrapped up in their arms.

"I was scared stiff the whole time!" her mother said. "But I'm so proud of you! And Wallace!" Wallace shook his head and did a kind of bow.

"Unbelievable!" was all her father said.

The crowd settled down once more as the announcer told them about the trophy awards after the barbecue. Jimmy appeared and grabbed Caroline by the arm. For a second, he seemed about to hug her in his excitement, then stopped at the last moment.

"That was really amazing," he said, grinning.

"Thanks," Caroline said at last. She was saying it to everybody. Ian walked up too, looking tired and stiff, but beaming at her.

"Pretty good, Owen. But I'll get you next time."

"You don't stand a chance," Jimmy said, laughing. Ian just looked at him, still smiling. Caroline felt as though she were somehow split in two, part of her experiencing the scene, another part just watching, as if it were all happening to someone else. It would take a little time for it all to register. People were shaking her hand, patting her on the back, congratulating her. She recognized a few faces, one of them Rob Enns, acting like a gentleman after all.

Then one face loomed close to her, one that she knew she had seen before, but wasn't sure where. The woman stood out from the others in a way Caroline couldn't quite place. She was tall and thin and seemed perfectly calm surrounded by a sea of excited spectators. The woman held out her hand, and Caroline took it.

"Congratulations!" the woman said. "That was a magnificent ride."

"Thank you," Caroline said softly, at last putting a name to the face. The woman turned to Caroline's parents and shook hands with each of them.

"You must be very proud of her."

"Thanks," her father said. "We are." Caroline saw the same look on both her parents' faces. They had recognized the woman as well.

"I'll let you enjoy your moment," she said to Caroline. "But I'd really like to speak to you and your parents later, if I may. I wonder if you've given any thought to your future in riding?"

With that, the woman smiled and stepped back into the crowd.

"Do you know who that was?" Ian said.

Jimmy looked at them, then at the departing woman. He seemed bewildered by the commotion. "No. Who was she?"

"You don't know?" Ian said, looking incredulously at Jimmy.

"Should I?"

"That was Ann Martin," Caroline said. She saw by the look on Jimmy's face that he still didn't get it. "You know! Ann Martin! Glennmohre Stables?"

Jimmy shrugged. He still didn't know what the big deal was.

"Only the biggest stable in all of Alberta. Maybe all of Canada!" Ian said. "Did you hear that? She wants to talk to you!"

"Why would Ann Martin want to talk to us?" Caroline's mother said. Her father shook his head, but he and Caroline made eye contact and she knew they were thinking the same thing. Caroline shrugged instead of answering her mother. But they had all heard what Ann Martin had said. She wanted to talk to Caroline.

Talk about her future!

4

Glennmohre Stables

Caroline could barely keep still in the back of her parents' van as they drove up the long driveway to Glennmohre Stables. She kept shifting about, looking out one side then out the other as something else caught her eye.

For as long as she could remember, she had driven past these stables and the magnificent pastures that surrounded them. Glennmohre was situated in a deep valley, and the rolling hills circling it were covered with immaculate rows of white fences, behind which were always dozens of beautiful horses.

"Try and keep still!" her mother said, watching her. "We're almost there."

"I know," Caroline said. "But I don't want to miss anything!"

Her parents shared a smile as her mother turned to face the front again. The driveway leading up to the stables was wide and lined with high spruce trees. At Christmas, the trees were always covered with lights, which gave the grounds a fairyland effect.

"Remember when I was little," Caroline said, staring at the trees up close for the first time, "and I used to make you guys drive me here at Christmas?"

"Yes," her mother said. "We remember. Every Christmas Eve we had to drive by here so you could see the lights and the horses. You used to think that Santa lived here."

Her father nodded. "Maybe she was right. Take a look at this."

Caroline and her mother turned to the front and immediately saw what he meant. As they rounded the last part of curving road, the main house slowly came into view. Surrounded by trees, it had never been clearly visible from the highway. Caroline could only stare. The house was something out of a movie, or a fairy tale.

It had two storeys, with a high roof and wide, jutting dormers. A landscaped garden seemed to flow around it, flowers and bushes springing out behind carefully placed rocks and pools of water. The garden and the house both followed the natural contours of the landscape, creating the illusion that they had grown there naturally, that they weren't manmade. The house itself was old, but well cared for, with modern windows added to the facade. On one side was a conservatory and through its glass walls, Caroline could see that the garden continued inside the house, where it was protected from the elements. Two fieldstone chimneys seemed to grow out of the thick log siding and tall, lush fir trees nestled next to the house, standing on guard to protect it. Behind it, the peaks of the Rocky Mountains were plainly visible.

Her father parked their van in the circular driveway out front. All three of them emerged, looking around, trying not to gape.

"Wow," was all her father could say. Caroline nodded. The place was perfect. She saw a huge carved sign above the doorway of the house. It read "Glennmohre Stables" in old-fashioned print. Underneath it, in smaller letters, were the words, "Caide Mille Failte."

"What does that mean, Dad?" Caroline asked. Her father was full of useful (and sometimes useless) trivia. His gymkhana explanation was a good example of how reliable it could be.

He shrugged, reading the sign himself. "Who knows. Looks like Latin."

"Actually, it's Gaelic," a woman said. Caroline looked beneath the sign and saw Ann Martin walking down the wide front steps of her home. Another woman, much older and dressed in business clothes years out of style, tried to keep up. The second woman carried heavy files full of papers and it was obvious that she wanted Ann to look at them. Ann stopped and turned to the woman, saying something quietly to her. The woman nodded and retreated back inside the house. Despite the interruption, Ann's entrance was magnificent. To Caroline, she fit perfectly with her surroundings. She wore high leather boots, riding breeches and a bowler-shaped hat, the kind Caroline had seen people wear at English-style horse events. She used to think they looked a little goofy, but somehow Ann Martin managed to carry it off. Elegant was the best word to describe her, Caroline thought. It wasn't a word she had used to describe anyone before.

"My grandfather built this place nearly a hundred years ago. He wanted to turn the land into another Scotland."

Ann walked up to her parents and shook their hands firmly as she spoke, and Caroline couldn't take her eyes off her. There was something about her that was striking. She was older than Caroline's parents and her hair was mostly silver. She was very thin, her skin lightly lined. Caroline guessed that Ann hadn't changed a great deal since she was a girl.

"Thank you for stopping by at such short notice," Ann said to her parents.

"Thanks for inviting us," Caroline's mother said. Her mother was nervous. It was as if they had suddenly been dropped in a foreign country: no one knew exactly how to behave. Then Ann turned to face Caroline, smiling and holding out her hand. They shook and Caroline's mind raced as she tried to think of something to say.

"What's it mean?" Caroline asked at last, indicating the sign once more. Ann turned back to look at it.

"A hundred thousand welcomes. Rather ironic, since grandfather was a bit of a snob. He never welcomed anyone. Glennmohre is also Gaelic. It means 'Great Valley.' At least that part is accurate."

There was an awkward pause, as everyone waited for someone to say something.

"It's quite a spread you have here," Caroline's father said at last. "I've always wondered what it was like. Close-up."

"The house is lovely," her mother said quickly.

"It *is* nice, isn't it? But I can't take any credit. I was just born into it."

Caroline was about to speak. She had never admitted it to anyone, especially not her friends, but she had always had a secret interest in show jumping. The reason she had never admitted it was that she knew what her friends thought of the sport. It was a little too fancy, a hobby for spoiled rich kids. But there was something about it that had always fascinated her. So far, the closest she'd ever been to a real show was television or books.

She also knew a lot about Ann Martin. In particular she knew that Glennmohre Stables had been just another small breeding stable until Ann took it over from her father. Now it was one of the largest in Canada, known all over the world. It had already bred four Olympic champions.

"Would you like to see inside?" Ann asked Caroline's mother. Her mother smiled even more broadly at the thought of going inside. Then she looked at Caroline.

"Maybe Caroline would like to see the horses first."

"Would you?" Ann asked.

"Well..." Caroline said. She was desperate to see the horses. She wanted to see the inside of the house too, but she had her priorities.

"Why don't we tour the stables, then have coffee in the house later?" Ann said. "I think I may have something interesting to discuss." Everyone nodded and Ann led the way.

"Glennmohre actually takes up over three hundred acres," Ann explained as she led the tour. "But the stables and grounds only take about forty."

Only forty, Caroline thought. That sounded like quite a lot to her. Ann continued her little lecture as they walked through the grounds. Glennmohre had two outdoor arenas and one indoor. It had its own veterinary clinic and a full-time staff of two doctors and their assistants. Caroline had never seen a clinic designed only for horses before. When Wallace had been sick, which was rare, the vet always came out to the acreage.

In the centre of the hospital was a large surgery. There was a huge steel platform sitting upright in the centre of the cold, sterile room.

"What's that for?" Caroline's mother asked Ann.

"It's the operating table," Ann replied. All of them were surprised. "We strap the horse to the table while it's upright like this. Once in position, the motors underneath lower the platform to a flat surface that allows the surgery to proceed."

"This place is better equipped than some hospitals I've seen," Caroline's father said, looking over the sparkling facilities.

"We think the horses are worth it. Wouldn't you agree, Caroline?"

Caroline only nodded. She was equally impressed.

The stables were huge and well ventilated. Each horse, and there were dozens of them, had its own private stall with fresh water running constantly into a trough. Each horse's name was engraved on a plaque on the door of the stall.

"There are pipes underneath the tiles," Ann explained, indicating the floor of the barns. "In the summer we run cold water through them to cool them, and in winter, hot water to keep them warm."

Like the surgery and the rest of the grounds, the stables were all clean and airy. Caroline saw several people, mostly teenagers scurrying around, cleaning.

"Pretty nice," her father said. "When can we move in?"

Caroline watched as Ann smiled, even though she'd probably heard the joke a thousand times before. When she turned away to speak to one of the stable hands, both Caroline and her mother slapped her father on an arm. He looked puzzled, no doubt wondering what he had done to embarrass them this time.

Ann finished with the stable hand and looked at her watch. "I believe the riding class is about to begin," she said, turning back to them. "How would you like to see some students in action?"

***

Caroline thought that the indoor arena had to be the biggest building she'd ever been in. It was like standing in the centre of the Millarville Paddock, only with a roof over you!

There were jumps set up in the centre of the arena placed in different positions. Ann pointed to the jumps as they walked around.

"These are all vertical or single jumps," she said. "Do you know what any of them are called?" she asked Caroline.

"Well," Caroline said, pointing to a large one that looked like a section of fence. "I think that's a wall. And that one's a cross pole and that one with the flower pot kind of thing is a narrow brush."

"Very good," Ann said. "I had a feeling you knew more than you were letting on." She leaned closer to Caroline, smiling, lowering her voice, "You probably checked me out, too. Didn't you?"

Caroline shrugged and looked away, embarrassed. Ann looked amused.

"Where'd you learn all that?" her mother asked.

"Just reading and stuff," Caroline said shrugging again.

"And you told us you thought horse jumping was for sissies!"

"Dad!" Caroline said, even more mortified. She may have said it, but she would never have said it in front of Ann.

"It's okay," Ann said. "The uneducated see the funny pants and the jackets and think that it's only a sport for rich snobs who want to show off. Let's get out of the way and watch the class. Maybe you'll have a different opinion."

She led them to an elaborate private booth where they had a good view of the entire arena. The booth was equipped with its own mini-kitchen, and Ann served coffee for herself and Caroline's parents. Caroline drank iced tea.

A group of about fifteen kids on horseback, all near Caroline's age, emerged through a side entrance. They were dressed similarly to Ann. All of them wore the bowler hats that were actually helmets, designed to protect a rider in case of a fall. A man followed them on foot and began shouting out instructions. He was short and stocky and wore riding breeches and a faded, baggy tweed sportscoat. He also wore one of the low caps she had sometimes seen British men wear. As she listened to him, she realized he was British, recognizing the thick accent.

"That's Sam Burke," Ann said. "He's our head groom and also teaches the jumping class."

"Don't you teach?" Caroline asked.

"I used to. Mainly equitation. These days, the Stable keeps me far too busy. Besides, Sam's much more experienced in jumping than I ever was."

The four of them looked on as Sam put the group of ten kids through a gruelling work-out. As they watched, Ann explained to Caroline and her parents what was happening, telling them the point of each exercise. A girl of about twelve or thirteen caught Caroline's eye. Sam was tough on all of the students, but he seemed to be particularly hard on her. Caroline admired the girl's silent determination.

After several runs through the course, she could see that both the girl and her horse were tired. Sam ordered them through once more.

"Why's he being so mean to her?" Caroline said at last.

"He's not being mean, Caroline," Ann replied. "Sheryl is a good rider. She has a lot of potential, but she doesn't put her heart into it the way she needs to if she ever wants to be a champion."

Caroline still thought that Sam was being too harsh. She was also nervous for the girl, watching her as she circled around to begin her next attempt. She was simply too tired to guide her horse properly. Caroline sat forward, tense, holding her hands under her chin and rocking.

"What are you seeing?" Ann asked Caroline, as she rocked nervously back and forth.

"She's tired. So's her horse. She's going to make more mistakes."

They watched as Sheryl barely made the first two jumps. Caroline became very agitated. She glared at Sam, who still shouted harsh commands at the girl. As she approached the next jump Caroline nearly stood up; she could see immediately what was about to happen.

"What?" Ann asked her, seeing her tension increase.

"The girl is slouching and not concentrating. She's letting her horse lead, not controlling him."

Ann seemed pleased with her observations and sat back to watch once more. As the horse jumped, it seemed to lose momentum in mid air. Its feet crashed into the poles, knocking them free. Sheryl was thrown off and landed heavily on the dirt floor. Several of the other students made a move to help her up.

"Leave her be!" Sam shouted. His thick accent made it hard to understand him. He walked closer to Sheryl. "Are you hurt?"

The girl was up on one knee, adjusting her helmet. She shook her head and stood up, dusting herself off.

"Good," Sam said. "Then get back on."

"The poor girl," Caroline's mother said. "Why doesn't he just let her stop?"

"He can't let her finish with a mistake. She has to force herself to get back on and finish the jump."

Caroline disagreed. "That girl did her best. She and her horse should have time to rest before she gets back on."

"In competition, neither of them has that luxury."

Sheryl rubbed her lower back, then swung her arms as if trying to get the kinks out. She walked slowly over to her horse, mounted him and finished the course. When she was through, Sam and the others applauded her performance.

Caroline was impressed. She wondered if she would have had the strength to go on after being treated that way.

"So," Ann said as the students began to file out of the arena. "Do you still think that jumping is just for sissies?"

Caroline shook her head. After what she had seen, she knew that wasn't true. Ann smiled approvingly and leaned back in the chair, taking a delicate sip of coffee.

"Good. Because I think you have the talent to become a real champion. And I want you to join my team."

5

A Way with Horses

I just don't know," Caroline's mother said as she sipped her coffee. The four of them now sat in the sunroom of the main house. Caroline was too nervous to sit with the others. Instead she paced back and forth, looking out the huge windows at the paddocks and the horses. Sheryl, the girl she had seen jump in the arena, walked by, carrying her saddle. She saw Caroline in the window and smiled, waving to her. Caroline waved back, wondering how the girl could smile after what she had just been through.

"It's just such a dangerous sport," Caroline's mother said, continuing. "I'm worried about her being hurt."

"Mom!" Caroline said. "I've been riding since I was eight. I've fallen off lots of times! I've never been hurt yet."

"I can't deny there's risk involved. But there's a chance of being hurt in any sport," Ann replied.

"It's not just that," her mother said. "I don't know a lot about jumping. But I do know that it's expensive. I really don't think we could afford—"

"Let's not talk about that side of it right now," Caroline's father said, cutting his wife off brusquely. "It's just a big commitment."

"Let me tell you something," Ann said, sitting forward, resting her elbows on her knees. "I know that Caroline has tremendous potential. I was stunned by what I saw her accomplish with no formal training. And it's not just that. You heard her this morning. She knew exactly what was about to happen to that student, before it happened. She has that special empathy for horses that only the best riders possess. 'A way with horses' was the phrase my grandfather used to describe it. I believe that with my help she could go far in the sport. Very far."

It felt strange to Caroline to be just standing there, listening to them debate her future as if she wasn't in the room. But she knew her parents well enough to realize that she had to keep quiet, to let them think this through.

"To prove to you that I mean what I say, let me propose this. I'll let Caroline join my school, free of charge. If she proves to be as talented as I predict, then she can join my team. In fact, even Jump Alberta is well within her potential."

"Jump Alberta!" Caroline whispered. "You mean this year?"

"Of course," Ann replied. "As part of my school you have free access to any of the horses, and the Stable pays most expenses in competition."

Caroline dropped down into a chair, trying to grasp what Ann had said. Jump Alberta was the highest competition for her age group. She could hardly believe someone like Ann Martin felt she had the talent to compete. And compete this fall!

Caroline's parents looked at each other, and she saw her father's face redden, the way it did when he was upset about something. He put down his coffee cup and stood.

"I think my wife and I better discuss this alone."

"Dad!" Caroline said. She knew that there would be no more discussion.

"I'm sorry, Mr. Owen," Ann said, standing up as well. "Did I say something wrong?"

"Look. I appreciate you inviting us here and letting Caroline see the horses. And your offer. But we're not exactly poverty stricken. If my daughter has the potential that you say and if lessons are something she really wants, we'll find a way to make it happen. Ourselves."

Caroline was about to speak again, but she turned away, furious at her father's stupid pride. She looked across the lane to the paddocks again and saw the teenage grooms busily working. And that's when the idea struck her.

"May I make a suggestion?" Caroline said, turning back to the adults staring at each other in uncomfortable silence.

"Of course you can," her mother said.

"What if I worked to pay my way?"

"What do you mean work?" her father said. "You're too young to get a job."

"And where would you work, anyway?" her mother added.

"Here. At the stables. I could clean the stalls, groom the horses. All kinds of stuff."

Her parents looked at each other again, and Ann smiled.

"I don't know..." her father said softly.

"Come on, guys!" Caroline said, trying hard not to be completely exasperated with them. "I've been doing it every day with Wallace, haven't I?"

"I think it's a brilliant compromise," Ann said. Her parents still looked hesitant.

"You know, I just realized," Ann said. "All this debating and no one has even asked what you want. Do you want to learn to jump?"

"More than anything!" Caroline said. As she said it, she knew that it was something she had just realized herself.

"Well," her father said at last. "If it's something she really wants, I guess we can try it for a while."

Caroline ran over to him and hugged him. Then she hugged her mother. All that was left now was for them to work out the details. Ann offered to call that evening, once everyone had had time to think. She led them out the door, back through the house to the driveway. As Ann walked them back to their car, she slowed down a little to speak quietly to Caroline. "You know I said you had a way with horses?"

Caroline nodded.

Ann smiled. "Somehow I think you have a way with adults, too."

***

Caroline took in a deep breath, smelling the fresh scent of the spruce and fir trees. It was the best evening of her life: she had been invited to take lessons at Glennmohre and she was riding along the winding forest paths with her horse and her two best friends.

She spoke very little, just listened to them ramble on about sports and horses. And girls. She had noticed that both of them spoke a lot more about girls than they used to.

"Why are you grinning so much?" Ian asked as the path widened enough for him to ride beside her and Wallace.

She had been dying to tell him all day, but didn't know how he would react. She knew what he thought about show jumping.

"Nothing," she said.

"You sure are happy about something," Jimmy said, riding a metre or so ahead.

"Well…" she began, wondering how to tell them, "I got a job today."

"A job?" Ian said, surprised. "What kind of job?"

"Taking care of horses at a stable."

"Which stable?"

"I bet I know which one," Jimmy said. "It was that Glen-something one. Right?"

Caroline didn't answer, she just grinned wider.

"Is that what Ann Martin wanted to talk to you about after the GK?" Ian asked.

Once more, Caroline didn't answer, she only pressed her legs gently on Wallace's sides, to spur him on. All three of them began to quicken the pace.

"So when do you start?"

"Tomorrow."

"That's fast. How long do you work?" She shrugged. "I'm not sure. Probably all day."

"Every day?" Jimmy asked.

Caroline nodded.

"Wow. I guess we won't see much of you."

Caroline looked at him, her grin slipping a little. It was the first time she had thought of it that way.

"Glennmohre Stables, huh. I bet they pay pretty good, don't they?"

Caroline looked away again, knowing that she had to tell them the whole story. "Actually," she began, "it doesn't pay much."

"So how much does it pay?"

"Nothing."

"Nothing?" they said in unison.

"I get other things besides money."

"Yeah? Like what?" Ian asked.

Caroline hesitated only a moment. "Like lessons."

"What kind of lessons?" Jimmy asked.

Ian looked a little puzzled, and she saw his mind was racing, figuring it all out.

"Don't tell me!" he said. "No way! Not you!"

Caroline said nothing. Jimmy looked back and forth at them.

"What?" he asked at last.

"Caroline's going to be one of those fancy horse jumpers!"

"She is?"

Jimmy had slowed down now, trying to ride beside the others. The trail was a little too narrow, so he had to twist his body almost completely around to see them.

"I thought you guys thought they were all spoiled wimps or something," he said.

"Maybe I did think that," Caroline said. "But that was before I actually saw them training. You should see how tough it is. And the horses! The horses are gorgeous!"

"And so are the hats! And so are those little red coats and fancy pants they get to wear!" Ian said, laughing. "I can just picture you wearing that outfit, jumping over an old fence at the Paddock next year! You'd look real nice!"

"Oh yeah?" Caroline said, getting angry now. "At least I can stay on a horse!"

"Oh yeah?" Ian said, sounding surprised, then angry himself. "At least I don't think I'm the best thing that ever got on one!"

"Hey, you two!" Jimmy said. "Take it easy!"

"Why don't you both just take off!" Caroline said. She was too mad to think straight. "Maybe you can find Allison Gates and some of her pals hanging out at the make-up counter!"

"Maybe we should," Ian said. "At least they look like girls!"

Caroline just glared at him. Ian had gone too far. She squeezed Wallace's sides even harder and he galloped off. She felt her eyes sting and hoped it was only because of the brisk wind.

***

It was hours later, and the sun had already dipped behind the mountains. Caroline had just finished grooming Wallace and was putting his night blanket on.

"I'm glad you can't talk, Wall," she said. "It seems that it's mostly dumb things that people say."

She still felt hurt and angry about the fight with Ian earlier. These feelings mixed in with her excitement and worry about starting at the Stables tomorrow and her guilt about not spending as much time with Wallace. She felt very confused.

Wallace seemed to sense her mood. He was quieter than usual and didn't squirm too much when she groomed him. He even accepted the blanket, although usually he fought it, knowing that he was now cooped up till morning. As she checked his haynet and water, she heard the sound of hooves on her driveway.

Caroline left the paddock and walked along the fence, watching Ian ride up. He looked very uncomfortable, almost as uncomfortable as she felt.

"Hi," he said.

"Hi," she replied.

"What're you doing?"

What's it look like I'm doing, she wanted to reply. Instead she shrugged. "Putting Wall away."

Ian nodded and pushed his battered straw hat back from his forehead.

"So. You looking forward to work tomorrow?"

"I guess."

"You riding there?"

"I was planning on it." The Stables were about a ten-kilometre ride, through trails that she knew well. She had to cross only one main road on the way. Ian fidgeted on his saddle, and took a long time checking his reins.

"If you want, maybe I can ride with you, part way," he said at last.

"I don't know. I have to be there at eight," she said, her voice noncommittal.

Ian shrugged. "I don't mind. If it's okay and stuff."

"I guess."

He nodded, and pressed the reins against Buck's neck, turning him about. "I better get home. See ya in the morning."

She watched him slowly ride back down the path, appearing and disappearing as he passed under the lights.

"See ya," she said. She knew that Ian had just apologized. But she felt that something else had happened between them this afternoon. Something more important than just another argument. Somehow, she still felt hurt.

6

English Style

Caroline felt a twinge of guilt as she left Wallace in the paddock. He looked back at her as she walked away, as if wondering where he was and why she was leaving him there alone, surrounded by strange horses.

Ian had left her at the front gates of the Stables. They had spoken very little on the ride over and what they had discussed was pretty trivial.

Ann was waiting for her at the first stable as she had promised yesterday. Today, instead of breeches and high boots, she wore jeans with leather chaps and jodhpur boots. Caroline wondered if she always dressed as if she were about to go riding. She had yet to see her on a horse.

"Good morning, Caroline," she said briskly, as she walked up to her. "All ready to begin, I hope."

"I can hardly wait!" Caroline replied.

"You'll start every day, Monday to Friday, at eight," Ann said, walking back to the stables with her. "The grooms will find lots of work for you, I'm sure. Classes will be for three hours each day. On your own at first, until you've caught up enough to join the regular classes. You'll start off with basic equitation."

Caroline was disappointed. She had hoped she would start jumping right away. Ann must have seen it in her eyes.

"Don't worry. You'll be jumping soon enough. You've studied equitation on your own, haven't you?"

Caroline nodded.

"I thought as much. I could tell by the way you sat on your horse and the way you handled him. You've learned a lot on your own. Now it's time to fine-tune you."

Ann introduced her to the grooms, most of whom were only a few years older than Caroline, high school or university students making money over the summer.

"Don't work too hard," Ann said as she left Caroline with the others. "Sam and I will be back after lunch to start your lessons."

"Don't work too hard!" one of the girls said after Ann left, imitating her walk and voice. The imitation was pretty good, too, Caroline noticed, even though the girl was short and stocky with thick black hair and ruddy cheeks. She looked nothing like Ann. The others laughed, watching her performance, and Caroline noticed the laughter wasn't friendly. So far, Ann had seemed very pleasant. She wondered why the grooms seemed so willing to sneer at her behind her back.

Caroline was quickly introduced to everyone, but she could only remember one name. Maggie was the black-haired girl. She handed Caroline a pair of work gloves.

"So," Maggie said, looking Caroline over. "You look kind of young to be working, even by Ann's standards."

Caroline felt a little awkward. They all stood staring at her, waiting.

"I'm just working to pay for riding lessons. Ann asked me to join her team."

The others looked at each other and grinned again.

"Isn't that just swell of her?" Maggie said, looking at the others. "Good old Ann. Always willing to help out the peasants."

Caroline felt more and more uncomfortable. She just wanted to get to work.

"Have you met Sam yet?" one of the others, a boy with a bad case of acne, asked.

"No. But I saw him teach a class yesterday."

"You're in for a treat, then," the boy said.

"Ever muck out a stable before?" another girl asked, showing her where the shovels and pitchforks hung.

"I clean up after my own horse every day," Caroline replied.

"Wait till you clean up after one hundred," Maggie said. "It's a whole new experience!"

***

Caroline lay on a huge haystack, too exhausted to move. Every muscle in her body ached and the lunch her mother had prepared for her lay untouched in its wrapper. She had managed to sip only half of the apple juice she had packed. Even her lips hurt.

She was leaning against the wall of a stable, watching Wallace in the paddock. Another young gelding had already become drawn to him, never letting him move more than a few metres away. The gelding's name was Stirling, one of the grooms had told Caroline. None of them liked taking care of him. He was too high strung and unpredictable.

On impulse, she had decided to lead Stirling out of his stall and into the same paddock as Wallace. After a few comforting words and a treat of fresh sweetgrass, Stirling seemed to trust her. Wallace got along with anyone, and the younger horse was quickly attached to him.

"Hi up there!" a voice called out.

Struggling hard, Caroline managed to make it to a sitting position. A girl stood at the base of the haystack, smiling up at

her. The girl had short blond hair and big blue eyes. She
looked very familiar, but Caroline took a moment to place her.
It was Sheryl, the girl who had fallen from her horse in the
arena yesterday.

"I saw you yesterday in the arena, didn't I?" the girl
asked.

Caroline nodded. Even that hurt. And she had to ride in
less than forty minutes!

"Are you related or something?"

"Related?"

"To Miss Martin."

"Me? I just work here."

"Really?" Sheryl said, looking surprised. "Mind if I join
you up there?"

Caroline was too tired to care. Besides, the girl seemed so
cheerful, it was a pleasant change from all the miserable faces
she had put up with this morning. None of them seemed
happy working there. She wondered why they bothered if it
upset them so much.

"I'm Sheryl Innis," she said as she plunked herself down
beside Caroline. Sheryl was the complete opposite of
Caroline. Her hair was fine and so blond it was almost white.
Her skin was pale and lightly freckled, and her eyes were a
deep blue. Caroline felt stocky and coarse next to her. Sheryl
wore jeans and a simple denim shirt, almost identical to what
Caroline wore, but somehow she looked different. The clothes
fit her in a way that Caroline couldn't quite place. She also
wore a pair of riding boots that Caroline had once seen in a
catalogue. The boots were worth more than her best saddle.

"I'm Caroline Owen."

"You really just work here?" Sheryl said, still smiling, but
looking a little confused.

"Well, I'm also going to take jumping lessons."

"Yeah? That's great. How old are you?"

Caroline thought it was a rather unusual thing to ask straight out like that.

"Twelve," she replied.

"Me, too! At last I'll have someone my own age in class. The other kids think they're so mature!"

Sheryl seemed nice, but Caroline was just too tired to make conversation right now.

"I thought you must be a relative or something. I've never seen anyone invited up to the main house before. I think my parents were a little insulted that they weren't invited when I started riding here." All of this came out in a breathless rush that Caroline took time to decipher. She wondered if she was supposed to be honoured by Ann's invitation; once more she was too tired to care.

"So what makes you so special?"

Caroline shook her head. "I'm not. Ann saw me at a gymkhana on the weekend and asked me if I wanted to take lessons here."

"She asked *you*?" Sheryl asked. "Just like that?"

Caroline nodded. Sheryl looked even more impressed. "Wow! Have you any idea how long the waiting list is to get into this school?"

"I didn't even know there was one."

"Boy! I really can't wait to see how you ride!"

Caroline thought about how every muscle ached and the agony of getting on a horse. "Me too," she said weakly. Sheryl laughed as if what she had just said was hilarious.

"Stirling looks like he made a friend," Sheryl said, looking over at where the two horses stood.

"That's Wallace. He's my horse. I figured he'd calm Stirling down. He seems pretty jumpy."

"Stirling's my horse."

"Oh, sorry!" Caroline said, embarrassed. "I didn't mean anything."

"It's okay," Sheryl said. "He *is* pretty jumpy. He usually won't let anyone but me take him out of his stall."

There was a long pause in the conversation. Caroline thought she had better say something, since Sheryl had done all the talking so far.

"I thought you rode really well yesterday," she said. "Sam was too hard on you, though."

Sheryl shrugged and grinned. She seemed pleased by the compliment. "Believe it or not, Sam was actually in a good mood yesterday. He's pretty tough on us and the horses, but he really knows his stuff."

She stopped and looked around, then slid along a little closer to Caroline.

"Did any of the grooms tell you why Sam lives in Canada now?" Sheryl had lowered her voice slightly, as if someone might overhear.

Caroline shook her head.

"Sam worked for some huge stable in England. Something really bad happened and he had to get out of the country. They say that Sam Burke isn't even his real name."

"Really?" Caroline asked. "What did he do?"

She couldn't help being curious. She usually got bored quickly when kids started gossiping like this, but Sheryl seemed to be a natural storyteller. Caroline wanted to listen despite herself.

"Who knows?" Sheryl replied. "Some say that he worked for a lord or an earl or something and he was caught mistreating an expensive horse. That's why he couldn't work in England any more."

"If that was true, why would Ann hire him?"

Sheryl shrugged. "Who knows? Maybe she got him to work cheap. Or maybe she's blackmailing him."

"Why would she do that?" The story was starting to get a little too unlikely.

"Who knows?" Sheryl said again. "But you should see the way she treats him sometimes, and he never says a word."

Caroline decided to change the subject.

"So. How long have you had Stirling?" This made Sheryl forget all about the Sam saga. They chatted for awhile about their horses. Too soon, Caroline had to leave to start her first lesson. She wanted to stay all afternoon with Sheryl; rarely had she hit it off with another person so quickly. Especially another girl.

"Maybe we can go for a ride or something later, if you want," Sheryl said as Caroline slowly made her way down the haystack.

"Maybe," she said, even though she knew she would be too sore to ride any more today.

"Where do you live?"

"My parents have an acreage just outside Millarville."

"Really? We have one in Red Deer Lake. We're practically neighbours!"

They exchanged phone numbers and Sheryl promised to call after supper to make plans. Caroline waved goodbye and headed to the arena, feeling nervous and excited all at once.

***

"No! No! No!" Sam shouted. Caroline tensed again, feeling her posture shift and Wallace begin to canter. For the first time in her life she hated riding and horses.

"All right, Sam!" Ann said, clapping him on the shoulder. Caroline saw that Ann was annoyed at him, but she concealed it quickly, smiling once again. "It's only her first lesson. Why don't you take a break?"

Sam looked at Ann, still red faced. He didn't say a word as he handed her the lunge line. Caroline and Sam exchanged a look as he let go. Up close, she saw that Sam was about the same age as her father, but the hair under his old cap was long and streaked with grey.

"I still think it was a mistake allowing her to ride her own horse. There's years of bad habits to break!"

"It was my idea for her to use her own horse," Ann said coolly. This seemed to shut Sam up. He looked down, avoiding eye contact with Ann.

Wallace snorted and pulled once more at the long lunge line, as if he knew he had just been insulted.

"As I said, Sam," Ann said slowly. "Why don't you take a break?"

Still not looking up at her, Sam turned to walk away. Caroline let out a sigh of relief once Sam had left the arena.

"Why is he so angry?"

"Sam's not angry, Caroline. He's a perfectionist. Don't worry. He may seem a little gruff, but all he wants is for everyone to be their best."

Ann continued where Sam had left off, showing her the proper way to sit and how to hold the reins to control her horse. The smaller, English-style saddle had taken some getting used to at first, but Caroline felt confident in it now. Both she and Wallace were still having problems with the new bridle and the English style of using the reins. Wallace was used to the reins pressed lightly against his neck, depending on which direction she wanted him to go. Now Caroline had to keep the reins tight in each hand and pull back on the left or right to direct him. Her wrists and arms were tired from holding them in such an awkward position. Wallace was smart and Caroline had never needed many riding aids to control him.

Caroline felt tired, sore and unsure of herself. She had thought she knew a lot about the fine points of riding, but there was so much more to know if she ever wanted to compete.

Finally, after nearly two hours, Ann told her that they'd done enough for one day.

"You did very well today, Caroline," she said as she flipped the reins over Wallace's head. "It won't take long at all to get you into top shape."

Caroline was too tired and too sore to reply.

"Why don't you go home now and have a nice long bath. I'll see you here again first thing."

Ann patted Wallace's shoulder and Caroline nodded and managed to say something in reply. All she thought of was the long ride home and the idea of sinking into a hot tub and never having to come out again.

7

The Trail Ride

How's it feel to be in the real class now?" Sheryl asked as she handed the body brush to Caroline. They were both in the stable, both still in their riding clothes, grooming their horses. Stirling and Wallace stood side by side, tethered to the wall as the girls worked.

Caroline shrugged. "Pretty good, I guess. It feels a little weird. All of you've been together for so long, I feel kind of lost."

"You fit in fine," Sheryl said, laughing. "Are you looking forward to your first event?"

There was a Young Riders competition at a stable near Canmore; Caroline was going, but only as a groom. Although she had been in classes for almost two weeks now, Ann felt she wasn't ready to compete just yet. Caroline was disappointed, but Sheryl agreed with Ann that Caroline should at least watch an event before entering one.

"Sure. I really want to see you and Stirling compete. I bet you'll do well."

"Let's hope so," Sheryl said. "Or my parents will be miserable the whole ride home." There was a lull in her usual enthusiasm. Caroline wanted to say something, but couldn't think of the right thing. Sheryl had just finished cleaning Stirling's feet and had bent down to examine his hooves for splits or other signs of stress.

"He needs a couple of new shoes," Caroline said, starting to vigorously brush Wallace's side. Sheryl looked at the feet again while Caroline showed her the tiny signs of wear.

"Hey, Caroline!" a voice shouted. Caroline and Sheryl turned to see who had called. Two boys from their class were leading their horses toward them. They were both fourteen and more than a little obnoxious.

"How about earning your keep and taking care of our horses here?" one of them said, holding the reins out to Caroline.

"Why don't you grow up, Brad?" Sheryl replied. He and his friend, Tom, just looked at her.

"That's what she's here for, isn't it?" Tom said. He seemed a little less interested in teasing the girls, but was following his friend's lead. Caroline stood, brushing her hair from her eyes, breathing hard from the exertion of grooming Wallace. She said nothing as the boys tossed her the reins, then walked off, laughing at some private joke. Sheryl stood up to help Caroline lead the horses to another stall.

"Those boys are such jerks!" Sheryl said, annoyed. Caroline had seen enough of her new friend over the past two weeks to know that it took a lot to make her angry. "Why didn't you say something to them?"

"What's the use?" This was one reason she wasn't completely happy with the riding classes. Except for a few kids who came from ordinary families, most of the others in the class treated her like Brad and Tom did, as a groom who had to work to afford lessons. At least she had made a real friend in Sheryl, which was good, since she hardly had any time to see her old friends these days.

Since she had started the regular classes at the beginning of the week, she now spent the afternoons working in the Stables. It was hard work, and the days were long, even with the other grooms helping.

"Do they go to your school?" Caroline asked Sheryl when they returned to their own horses.

Sheryl nodded. "And they've always been annoying."

Over the last few weeks they had told each other all kinds of things about themselves. At first they thought it strange that though they lived so near each other, they had never met before. Part of the reason was that Sheryl attended a private school.

"They're just jealous of you," Sheryl said as they began grooming again.

"Jealous? Why?"

"Because they know that you're Ann's favourite. And that pretty soon you'll be jumping better than either of them."

"I doubt that," Caroline said. Secretly, the compliment filled her with pride. She had been aware of the others in her class and how much talent they had. It was hard not to make comparisons.

"You're already better than me."

"No, I'm not!"

"Sure you are. And you know it, too!"

Caroline tried once more to protest, but neither girl was really convinced by her attempts. Try as hard as she could, Caroline couldn't control her urge to compete with everyone, even her friends.

"I don't mind," Sheryl said. "It's my parents' dumb idea for me to compete. I'd be perfectly happy just riding Stirling."

"I like competition," Caroline said. "There's just something about it that's exciting."

"I know. That's why you're better than me. Winning matters to you."

"It's more than just winning," Caroline said, offended. She wasn't that shallow.

Sheryl grinned at her, and Caroline's annoyance disappeared again. "Don't get all huffy. I didn't mean anything. I just think that you like the whole thing more than I do. There's nothing wrong with that."

Caroline was looking at her friend, ready to apologize, when something else caught her eye. She looked over Sheryl's shoulder and saw Ann approaching. Sheryl caught her glance and turned to see what she was looking at.

"Hello, girls," Ann said as she walked up to them.

Caroline felt a little like she had been caught doing something wrong by a teacher. Here she was grooming her own horse and chatting with Sheryl. It didn't matter that she had finished all her other work first; for some reason Ann still made her feel guilty.

"And what were the two of you chatting about, all huddled up like that?" She smiled, but the smile had a hard edge. More and more Caroline noticed something in Ann's manner that made her uncomfortable.

"Nothing, Miss Martin," Sheryl replied.

"Well," Ann said. "You seem to be taking good care of your horses."

"I've finished all my other work," Caroline said. She felt that she had to explain herself.

"I know you have. You've been working very hard, both in class and in the stable. I won't keep you long. There's something I need to discuss with you, Sheryl."

Sheryl and Caroline looked at each other.

"I'm taking some of my clients on a trail ride tomorrow. It should be rather fun. We're even bringing along my favourite caterer. I thought you might ask your parents to join me. You're invited as well, of course."

"Sure!" Sheryl replied, obviously pleased. Caroline guessed it must be important to be invited.

"Can Caroline and her parents come too?" Sheryl added quickly.

A strange blank stare crossed Ann's face, but only for a split-second. It was obvious that she hadn't expected this.

"Well," she said, thinking. "It was meant to be a rather intimate affair. I couldn't possibly fit three more in this late." She paused and looked at the girls, considering.

"I think I could perhaps accommodate you. But just you, Caroline. As much as I'd love to invite your parents, there simply isn't the room. That is, if you even want to attend."

"I'd love to come!" Caroline said. She had begun to feel a little left out.

"Where are we riding to?" Sheryl asked.

"I thought Kananaskis Park. It's a nice ride this time of year. Caroline will need written permission from her parents. I want to be ready to leave at nine tomorrow morning."

With that, Ann turned to walk away. Sheryl turned to Caroline.

"Kananaskis! That'll be really nice." She saw the look on her friend's face. "What's the matter?"

"I don't think Ann really wanted me along," Caroline said.

"So?" Sheryl said, shrugging. "She probably only invited us because one of her fancy clients cancelled on her. I've heard about Ann's trail rides. The food's supposed to be wonderful! Don't worry, we'll have a great time making fun of Ann's snobby friends."

Caroline relaxed a little. It *would* be fun. Tomorrow was supposed to be as nice as it was today, perfect riding weather. Then she had another thought.

"I just remembered. Ian and Jimmy asked me to ride with them tomorrow. I said no because I thought I'd be working."

"So explain. They'll understand."

"They'll think I'm just avoiding them. I almost never see them any more as it is."

"Don't worry. Besides, what're the chances they'll pick the exact same trails we do?"

Caroline nodded. There were hundreds of different trails and the chances were slim that they would be on the same one.

***

They were up early the next day. Sam and Ann were leading the pack and Sam was trying his best to be charming. He had tidied himself up. Even his accent wasn't so harsh.

"Make sure there's no creases in your saddle blankets," he said as he went along through the ranks of horses and riders, checking everyone's tack. "If the horse develops saddle-sores, you'll be walking home!"

Most of the riders laughed at his comment. Caroline wasn't sure if they knew he wasn't joking.

"He's so funny!" one of the riders exclaimed. She was a rather heavy woman in her fifties, wearing brand new and expensive riding clothes. "And I love his accent!"

Sam smiled at her, but the smile faded the instant he walked away to attend to the next horse. Caroline walked alongside him, helping him get the horses ready. It appeared she was along as a groom rather than a guest.

"Bloody poseurs!" Sam mumbled under his breath as he swung up into his own saddle. Caroline didn't understand the word, but she recognized the sentiment. "Let's get this circus on the road, shall we?" he said to Caroline softly. She nodded and ran back to Wallace who was at the end of the line with the other grooms and the catering wagon. It felt strange for Caroline to be sitting on her old saddle again. For the last two weeks, she had ridden exclusively on the smaller English-style saddle.

Together, Sam and Ann dug in their heels, spurring the horses back down the line of riders. Sam still wore his flat, wool cap, even though everyone else wore cowboy hats. To Caroline, he looked like an extra in a British comedy who had wandered onto the set of a western. "Okay, folks," he shouted."I think we're ready to push off. Let's take it slow and easy, all right?"

"And remember," Ann said, "we're all here to have fun!"

As Sam approached, Stirling started to snort and buck slightly. Caroline had to grab his bridle, afraid that he would bolt before Sheryl could get him under control. Sam pulled his horse back, worried that Stirling might kick him.

"That horse is a menace!" Sam snapped. His superficial charm was gone. "If it gets spooked like that on the trail, it'll cause the other horses to panic."

"Sheryl," Ann said, reining in beside her. "Are you going to keep your horse under control?"

"Yes, Miss Martin," she replied, looking embarrassed by Stirling's reaction. Caroline was curious, too. He had been relatively calm the last two weeks, especially when Wallace was near him. It was almost as if Sam made him nervous.

"All right, then," Ann said. "Be careful with him."

Sam was obviously not happy with Ann's decision. As always, he deferred to her meekly, if not willingly.

"I don't get it," Caroline said to Sheryl. "He's been so good lately."

"Maybe he hates Sam's cheap cologne," Sheryl said.

They rode slowly and in single file. It was a beautiful warm summer day, and Sheryl and Caroline quickly forgot about Stirling's reaction to Sam. They joked and laughed for the first hour, barely noticing their surroundings or the others on the ride.

It took them nearly two hours to reach the rapids of the Elbow River, on the edge of Kananaskis County. From here they could already see the mist in the air and hear the sound of the falls further to the southeast.

As they approached the falls, they heard someone shout.

"On your left!" a voice called out from behind. Someone was riding up and wanted to pass the slower-moving train of horses. Caroline barely took notice and didn't recognize the voice. It was already getting hard to hear anything but the sound of the rushing water.

Sam raised his hand to signal that he had heard and to get his group to pull over to the right to allow the other riders to pass. Caroline and Sheryl were near the middle and Caroline was too busy looking at the view to worry about the riders coming up. Then she heard Sheryl call out to her, as quietly as she could over the roaring water.

"Caroline. Take a look. They're pretty cute."

Caroline turned her head to the left, to see what she was talking about. Instantly she regretted the move. If she had kept staring out across the water, maybe they wouldn't have seen her. Her heart sank as she turned to see Ian and Jimmy ride up alongside her and Wallace. The boys said nothing, just glared at her as they trotted by. Caroline felt the colour drain from her face.

She had told them she was working. They would think she had lied. She knew that neither boy would want to speak to her again.

8

Learning to Groom

Caroline finally had a moment to herself and leaned heavily against the fence, watching the competition. There were dozens of people both in the crowd and behind the scenes, taking care of the horses. It had been a two-hour drive northwest to the stable near Canmore, inside Banff National Park, and she had been working non-stop since dawn.

She and the other grooms had been at the stable at six, shampooing, grooming and feeding the horses. She had carefully bandaged the tails and legs of her horses to protect them during the ride. She had hoped to ride to the arena with Sheryl, but had been stuck in one of the trucks with two other grooms instead.

"And now the winners will take their victory lap!" the announcer called over the loudspeaker. Caroline laughed with everyone else as a group of little girls, none more than eight or nine years old, trotted their horses around the arena. Theirs had been the first event, held on the flat, meaning that none of the riders had actually had to jump. Each of the girls held a certificate and a white saddle blanket, their prizewinnings.

As the girls trotted happily out of the arena, the next event was called. This was Sheryl's event. Caroline watched as her friend and a group of other riders moved up toward the gate.

Ann had just walked through with a group of important-looking people. As soon as she passed, Maggie began entertaining the others with an impersonation. Caroline no longer felt guilty about laughing along with them. She had begun to see another side to Ann, a colder, harder side, even though it was well hidden behind the polished demeanour.

Of all the grooms, Maggie was the only one who treated Caroline as an equal. Despite her rough exterior, Maggie was understanding and had a wicked sense of humour.

Caroline left Maggie and the other grooms and walked over to Sheryl, wanting to wish her luck. She slowed when she saw the two people standing with Sheryl, guessing they were her parents. They were dressed in casual clothes that fit impeccably and Caroline noticed that Sheryl looked a lot like her mother. The three of them were deep in conversation. At least, the parents were. Sheryl seemed just to be listening. When they paused for a moment, Caroline saw her chance to interrupt.

"Hi," Caroline said as she walked up. Sheryl seemed relieved at the interruption.

"Hi," Sheryl answered. "Ann finally let you have a break?"

"Only a short one." She saw Sheryl's parents look at her, wondering who had interrupted them. Sheryl introduced her.

"Oh. So you're Caroline," her mother said. She had the same blond hair as Sheryl, a shade or so darker and cut even shorter. Sheryl had her mother's blue eyes. "Sheryl talks about you all the time. She says you're a wonderful jumper."

"So why aren't you in the event?" Sheryl's father asked. He was very tall and his hair was dark and perfectly cut. He reminded her of an actor, but Caroline couldn't think of which one.

"I'm not on the team yet. I'm here as a groom this week."

"That's nice, too," Sheryl's mother said. Caroline had been around grown-ups enough to know she was about to be dismissed. "You two can talk later. I think it's best if you're not distracted before the events, Sheryl."

"Mom, it's only Caroline."

"That's okay," Caroline said. "I better get back to my horses anyway."

Caroline and the other grooms minded the horses while the riders competed. She tied one horse up near the fence when she heard over the loudspeakers that it was Sheryl's turn in the ring.

It was a fairly simple course, and the jumps were set at three feet. Caroline watched her friend compete, looking at her for the first time with a new perspective, after her dozens of hours practising. Stirling, slightly nervous, seemed to relax as he headed for the first jump. Sheryl rode well, keeping her elbows tucked in, head up, her back and legs nicely positioned. Stirling did well too. The only fault occurred when he knocked the bar on the final jump and caused a moment of tension. Nothing fell.

Caroline saw the look on Sheryl's face, as she rounded the arena. She knew she had done well. As soon as she left the ring, her parents ran over to congratulate her. Caroline thought she'd wait until a better moment to add her congratulations.

All too soon, the competition was over. Ann's team had won first- and second-place ribbons. Sheryl, who was the second-place winner, was still grinning widely as she led Stirling out of the arena to the area where the trailers were parked. They spotted each other immediately and Sheryl ran over to hug her. Caroline was surprised — she had always been a bit uncomfortable hugging her friends — but Sheryl was so full of enthusiasm, it was hard not to join in. Caroline had already finished with most of her horses and grinned back as she slipped from Sheryl's arms and took Stirling's reins.

"Congratulations," she said. "You were great!"

Sheryl just shrugged. "It went pretty well, didn't it? And best of all, my parents won't be lecturing me about all the things I did wrong on the ride home."

Keeping her parents happy seemed more important to Sheryl than winning. Caroline could only guess at what that must feel like.

"Listen," Sheryl said. "What are you doing tonight?"

"Nothing, I guess." The last time she had seen Ian and Jimmy was on the trail. She still hadn't found the time to talk to them about it.

"Why not come over to my place and we'll hang out by the pool? You can even stay over if you want."

Although they had seen each other almost every day, neither had visited the other's home yet. From their long conversations, Caroline could imagine her friend's house. She had been dying to see if it was as wonderful as it sounded.

"Sure. Sounds like fun."

"Great. My Dad can come by and pick you up after supper."

Caroline suddenly felt a little worried, thinking of Sheryl and her father driving up to her ordinary house in their fancy car.

"Why not pick me up at the Stable? I'll probably be there late anyway."

"What about your stuff?"

"I'll ask whoever's driving the truck to detour by my place."

Sheryl nodded, then waved goodbye, rushing back to her father's car. They gave each other a final wave before she jumped inside. As they drove off, Caroline began to lead Stirling back to the trailer. Sam was in charge of the transport of the horses and he was helping Maggie and the others. They had done well in competition and Sam was in a good mood.

But as Caroline came up to the barn now, she saw Ann and Sam, standing apart from the others. Although Ann was speaking softly and Caroline couldn't make out what she was saying, it was obvious that she was giving Sam some kind of order. Judging by his reaction, Sam wasn't happy about it. He seemed to be trying to persuade her of something when Ann cut him off sharply. Creeping a little closer, Caroline began to make out the last of the conversation.

"I'm tired of excuses!" Ann said. "Just get all of the horses loaded. I want to be out of here within the hour!"

She strode off and Sam took off his cap, running a hand through his hair, taking a deep, weary breath. He was quick-tempered and Caroline saw that he was angry now.

He walked quickly back to the trailers, his mouth set in a grim line. Caroline was glad that she hadn't been seen.

"Look at the time! What have you been doing all day!" he yelled at Maggie, who was trying to lead a nervous horse into a trailer.

"Don't ask him politely!" Sam shouted again. "Show him who's boss!"

"We haven't even had time to clean the trailer properly," Maggie protested.

"So what? He'll just muck it up again!"

With that, he took the horse by the halter and used his riding crop to force it into the trailer. Caroline, who was leading Stirling toward the trailer, slowed down. Stirling, always extremely nervous around Sam, began to back away, nearly rearing up as Caroline tried to get him under control.

"Easy, Stirling!" she called out as calmly as she could. She didn't want Sam to see Stirling behave this way. He disliked the horse at the best of times. "Calm down, boy. It's okay!"

"What now?" Sam shouted, and Caroline knew who he was shouting at. He stomped over to them, snatching the reins from her hands.

"I'm tired of this horse acting up!" he said, pulling hard on the reins and trying to force Stirling to stop lurching about.

"You're hurting his mouth," Caroline cried, seeing him pull forcibly on the bit. Stirling, hurt and scared, tried to use his head to push Sam away. Sam was ready for the move and stepped aside quickly.

"Try to attack me, will you?" He brought the crop up again and struck Stirling hard on the shoulder, still dragging him toward the trailer.

"Stop it!" Caroline shouted, trying to grab his arm.

"Grow up!" He shook her off. "It's a working animal. Not a pet! The sooner you realize that, the better off all of us are. Do your job! Now untack him and get him ready to be loaded!"

He ordered the other grooms to help him trailer the horse. Kicking and fighting all the way, Stirling was finally locked up in the trailer. Sam looked pleased with himself as he secured the door.

"There's another lesson for you," he said to Caroline. "Free of charge."

He walked away, ignoring her as she glared at him. Sam ordered the drivers to get going, saying he wanted to be home for supper.

***

Caroline saw by the huge outdoor clock near the change room that it was past nine. She had been lying on a comfortable deck chair by the pool, feeling the still-warm evening air dry her. Sheryl lay on her stomach, looking at the reflections the water made on the high fences of her parents' yard. The house was huge, much too big for three people. But it was spectacular. From where she lay, Caroline saw the tall, arched windows that reached from the ground all the way up three storeys. Sheryl's mother had served them drinks and little fancy sandwiches. At Caroline's house her mother would have just told them to help themselves to whatever was in the fridge.

"What are you thinking about?" Sheryl asked. She had stopped staring at the water and was now staring at Caroline.

"Me? Nothing. I was just thinking how cool it must be to live in a house like this."

"It is pretty cool, I guess. As long as you only go where you're allowed. See what happens if you spill a coke on my mother's carpet!"

"She's not that bad! She seems really nice."

"She is, I guess. She just likes things to be a certain way. Including me."

Caroline didn't know what to say. She looked back at the house, seeing the warm glow of the lights behind the window. She wondered where Sheryl's parents were. Her own parents would have been checking on them every ten minutes, to make sure no one had drowned.

"Have you seen your friends lately?" Sheryl asked.

"Ian and Jimmy?"

"Yeah. Which one's the one with the light hair?"

"That's Ian."

"He's pretty cute, isn't he?"

Caroline looked over at her, wondering if she was serious.

"Ian? Cute? He's just a goof!"

Sheryl shrugged. She adjusted the strap on her brightly coloured bikini as she sat up. Caroline was wearing the same one-piece she'd had since grade six. It was starting to get tight.

"I think he's pretty cute. We should invite them riding one day."

"Sure. When I get a day off. And if they're still talking to me."

Caroline wasn't really sure if she wanted to introduce Sheryl to her old friends. She realized for the first time that she was embarrassed by them. They seemed so crude compared to Sheryl. Maybe she was wrong.

"How was Stirling going home?" Sheryl asked, changing the subject again. It was something she did often; sometimes if Caroline didn't pay close attention, she lost track of the conversation altogether.

She felt some of her anger coming back as she remembered taking the frightened horse out of the trailer and back to his stall. She had stayed with him for half an hour, trying to calm him down.

"He was fine," she said. She didn't want to tell Sheryl how Sam had handled Stirling. Instead, she asked, "Have you seen the way Sam treats his horses?"

"Sure. He's pretty rough. But he's like that with everything."

"I think he's too rough."

"He must know what he's doing. Besides, Ann has a lot of money tied up in her horses. She wouldn't let him do anything that was bad for them."

Caroline hoped that was true.

"I think Ann's going to let you jump in competition soon," Sheryl said.

Caroline nearly forgot her anger at Sam. "Really? Did you hear something?"

"No. But I've been watching you. And I saw her watching you a couple of times, too. I bet she'll ask you soon. Maybe even the next show."

Caroline felt her heart race a bit at the thought. She hoped that Sheryl wasn't just wishing.

"Maybe she'll even ask you for Jump Alberta."

"I don't know about that," Caroline said. Being allowed to jump was something that she could almost believe in, but jumping in the provincial finals was too much to ask for so quickly. Still, she remembered what Ann had promised her that first day.

"She'd be crazy not to let you. Anyone can see you're ready. And besides, you've got your competitiveness going for you. Maybe if I had your talent, I'd enjoy it as much as you do."

"You have talent. You won second place today!"

Sheryl stared at the pool again, her eyes clouding over slightly.

"I didn't win. My parents did."

9

A Promising Start

Caroline adjusted her coat and pulled at the waist of her riding breeches once more. They had a tendency to keep slipping down at the back, particularly when she was in the saddle. She looked at her teammates, especially Sheryl, who looked elegant in their custom-tailored riding suits. Caroline wore one borrowed from Ann's tack shop and felt she looked ridiculous. Once more, she adjusted the rolled-up cuffs of her bright red jacket. It was a replica of the kind worn by the national team and knowing that made her feel even more foolish.

"Stop fidgeting!" Ann said sharply to her. She had walked up to them, accompanied as always by Sam. "You have to concentrate on the course."

Caroline looked down at her, a little surprised by her tone. It was the first time that Ann's annoyance had been directed at her personally. She didn't like the feeling. Both Ann and Sam were more on edge than usual today, since the event was being held at Glennmohre.

Caroline was seated in Stirling's saddle, while Sheryl helped her make last-minute adjustments to his tack. Because of an insurance mix-up, Caroline wasn't allowed to ride Wallace in this event and Sheryl had offered her Stirling. Caroline wasn't sure if Stirling was the right choice; he only performed his best when Sheryl rode him. But she didn't know how to refuse her friend's offer. Ann hadn't seemed pleased, but she had said nothing.

"I'm still not sure about this," Sam said as he watched the girls make their adjustments. Stirling seemed a little jumpy with Ann and Sam so near. He seemed particularly nervous of Sam.

"Stirling is high strung," Sam continued. "I'd feel more comfortable if you rode a more experienced jumper."

"I'd really like to stick with Stirling," Caroline said. "We get along fine."

Sam looked doubtful, but didn't say anything more as he made a final check of the tack. He watched Caroline tap nervously on the saddle, then adjust her jacket once more.

"Try to relax," he said to Caroline. "This horse is nervous enough as it is without having you make things worse."

He patted Stirling's side and looked up at Caroline. His expression softened somewhat, as if he realized how harsh he sounded. "Don't worry. You'll be fine. I wouldn't let you jump if you weren't ready."

Caroline looked down at him, not knowing if he was actually smiling or if the sun in his eyes made him squint.

"He really knows how to encourage you, doesn't he?" Sheryl said as Sam and Ann walked over to the next horse.

"I just wish I didn't look so stupid," Caroline said. She wasn't really sure why she was so concerned about her appearence. Maybe it was just to stop worrying about the event.

"It's okay," Sheryl said. "You look fine." Brad and Tom snickered, obviously disagreeing with her appraisal.

The next rider was up now, one from a rival Stable. Caroline nudged Stirling into the dock, knowing that she was up next. She patted his shoulder and tried to relax him. It was a beautiful, sunny day with only a gentle breeze. Perfect for jumping. Caroline looked around and saw her parents in the stalls near the centre of the ring. They waved to her, but she couldn't wave back; it was time to think about the course. From her vantage point on top of Stirling, a few hands higher than Wallace, she could see the stables and the paddocks. She could even see Wallace prancing around in the distance.

"And next up is number 25!" the loudspeaker blared. "Caroline Owen aboard Stirling!"

Caroline was startled. She had barely heard the applause as the rider before her finished. She nodded as one of the attendants asked her if she was ready. Two little girls in helmets and breeches lifted the gate, giggling and proud of their responsibility, as Caroline nudged Stirling forward. She pushed him into a trot, circling the first jump, warming him up.

The course had seven jumps, the highest nearly three feet. They were jumps that she and Stirling were used to; the only difference was their placement and the addition of flowers to make the course more appealing for the spectators.

The first obstacle was a vertical, with three red and white poles set in brick posts. She tried to use very few aids in guiding Stirling to the first jump. He hesitated, jumping at the last possible moment and nearly knocking his feet on the rails. Caroline felt herself slide over the saddle too much and her elbows fly out. Stirling had jumped too far to the left. She spoke gently to him again, keeping his head down and his speed at an easy canter.

The next series of jumps were simple crossbars but there were three in a row, with only two and then three strides between them.

"Come on, Stirling," she said softly in his ear. "You're doing fine." She felt the tension in the horse, especially during the crowd's applause. She nudged his ribs gently with her legs as they approached the next jump. He leaped over the first of the triples, and she felt a lurch as he landed hard, urging him to the next and the next.

She calmed Stirling again as they rounded for the next jump. She felt the sweat trickle over her brow and the sleeves of her jacket begin to unravel. She knew she shouldn't worry about them now, all she should do was keep her seat and the proper two-handed grip on Stirling's reins. As they slid down, they made it hard for her to keep her grip. Quickly, hoping neither Ann nor Sam would see, she slowed Stirling slightly, rolled up one sleeve and then the other. It only broke her concentration for a few seconds; she was sure that Stirling's rhythm hadn't been affected.

Up next was a rounded wall, just a little over two feet high. It was a jump Stirling was used to; the only difference was the rows of bright red tulips planted at its base. She worried that the colour and the movement of the flowers in the breeze might spook Stirling.

He seemed fine until the last possible second, then something startled him and he jolted to a sudden stop. As Caroline slid out of her saddle, she grabbed onto his neck. She felt him begin to buck a little, trying to get her weight off him. Try as hard as she could, she couldn't hold on and she slid heavily to the ground, still trying to grasp at his mane.

She let go of the reins as she stood up, and Stirling immediately headed for the safety of the dock. Grooms ran out to capture him and lead him back to Caroline. As they approached, she took the opportunity to adjust her ill-fitting clothes once more.

Maggie handed the reins back to Caroline.

"Are you hurt?" she asked.

"Only my pride."

"Don't worry about it. You look great."

"Thanks," Caroline said, appreciating the compliment.

Maggie gave her a leg up, and Caroline eased herself back into the saddle.

"Whether you win or not today," Maggie said as she stepped back, "at least you don't have to muck out the trailers like the rest of us."

Caroline grinned at her and then urged Stirling into a trot.

"Stop being so nervous," she said soothingly to him. "After it's all over I've got a treat for you and your pal Wallace."

As she spoke, she felt the horse respond to her tone. She realized for the first time that she wasn't nervous any more. All she was concerned about now was her horse and helping him get over the last jumps. Slowly she picked up the pace as they approached the last two hurdles. Stirling left the ground in a perfect arc and she felt the familiar thrill while they were both briefly airborne. Stirling landed smoothly, and as Caroline headed back to the gate, she found herself smiling as she listened to the applause of the spectators.

"You were wonderful," Sheryl said as she ran up to them. "Both of you."

She rubbed Stirling's nose and he pushed himself against her shoulder. Caroline thought he looked relieved that it was over for the moment.

A few of her teammates also walked over to congratulate her. Brad and Tom nodded at her, not quite a compliment, but an acknowledgement that she had performed well. Not bad for just a groom, huh, boys, she thought to herself as she dismounted. She saw her parents had stepped through the gate.

"I thought I'd faint when I saw you grabbing that horse's neck!" her mother said as she hugged her.

"You did really well out there," her father said, giving her another hug. They seemed more excited than she was.

"You guys!" Caroline said as she pushed them away. "Enough already." Their enthusiasm was embarrassing; they had none of the reserve of her teammates' parents.

"Mind if we join you?" Jimmy called out from the other side of the fence. Ian stood beside him, looking a little uncomfortable. Caroline and Ian hadn't seen each other since the day they met on the trail.

"Sure," Caroline called back. She felt strangely excited to know they were here. It felt good to have all her friends around after her first real competition. Ian came up to her and she felt the same tension she had the last time she had seen him. She knew that he felt uncomfortable. He looked at her, then at his boots. Jimmy stared at her in a rather odd way, too.

"Aren't you going to introduce me?" Sheryl asked, sliding up beside Caroline. She quickly introduced them all.

"So you're Ian," Sheryl said as if she had never seen him before. "Caroline's told me a lot about you."

"Now you're in trouble," Jimmy said and punched his pal in the arm. Ian just grinned and blushed.

"Caroline was pretty good out there, wasn't she?" Sheryl said, breaking up the silence. "She's in second place right now."

"Not bad, Owen," Ian said. "You almost managed to stay on the horse."

Jimmy was grinning too, but his grin seemed a little forced. He was still looking at her strangely.

"What are you staring at?" Caroline said, suddenly embarrassed again. She adjusted the jacket, painfully aware that she looked ridiculous in it.

"I'm not staring," Jimmy said. "It's just you look different or something."

"Different?" she said. "How?" It hadn't been that long since she had last seen him. What was he talking about?

"I guess I never saw you wearing anything but jeans before."

She heard her father clear his throat loudly, to catch her attention.

"I guess we'll leave you kids alone now. We'll just go back to our seats."

Her parents left, sharing that same knowing look that Caroline had seen a thousand times before. She wondered what it was for this time.

"Are you jumping today?" Ian managed to say to Sheryl.

"Sure, I'm up after the next rider. Are you going to stick around?"

"Sure, I guess."

"I thought you didn't like jumping, Calder," Caroline said, teasing him. "You said it was only stuck-up phonies who jumped."

"I never said that," he protested, looking annoyed. They both knew he had.

"I think you did," Jimmy said.

Ian's face was bright red now.

Sheryl stepped forward. "Stop teasing him, you guys," she said. "How'd you like to meet my horse?" she asked him. Ian nodded, still embarrassed. Caroline and Jimmy watched as Sheryl led him away.

"So," Jimmy said. "Are you jumping any more today?"

"I'll have two more events at least. Then the judges pick the best."

"Me and Ian are going to stick around to watch. Okay?"

"Sure it's okay," Caroline said. She was still wondering why he seemed so tense around her. Was it really just because he had never seen her dressed like this before? They walked over to where Ian and Sheryl stood with Stirling. It was almost Sheryl's time to compete and she asked Caroline to give her a leg up.

"Good luck," Caroline said as her friend headed for the gate.

"Thanks. Why don't we all do something after the event?"

"Sure," Caroline said. Why was Sheryl worried about that now? She was supposed to concentrate on her jumping, not on what was happening tonight.

"Great." Sheryl glanced over at where her parents stood, grim-faced and tense. "Okay. Let's get this over with."

With those words, Sheryl gently nudged Stirling out into the arena as her name was called over the loudspeaker.

10

The Jump Alberta Team

The excitement in the arena was so thick, Caroline could almost taste it. The horses had picked up on it and paced nervously, tossing their carefully braided manes. Sam gave everyone a dark look as he rode along the column of students, displeased that they weren't keeping their horses in check. When Brad's horse took a sudden nip at his neighbour, Sam had seen enough.

"All right, people!" he shouted, the noise startling even his horse. As tense as she was, Caroline smiled at that, thinking Sam's horse should be used to his yelling by now. "Let's settle down, now!" Sam added.

They were all hot and tired from yet another gruelling work-out. Caroline wore her long hair up, letting the breeze from the open doors cool her neck. It was pouring rain, making it necessary for them to train inside, and the humidity in the arena made the air even thicker. As Jump Alberta approached, it was all that anyone thought about, and everyone wanted to make the final cut for the team. Sam had promised that Ann would announce her decision after today's lesson. As the moment approached, even the grooms slowly appeared from various corners of the arena, leaning on the boards or pretending to have some interest in a jump or the dirt covering the floor. Maggie, her black hair as wild as ever, was the only one not pretending. She stood against a post a few feet away, polishing a snaffle bit and waiting along with the riders.

Caroline and Sheryl looked over at her and she looked up, giving them a wink.

"Well," Sheryl said. "This is it, I guess."

"I guess," Caroline replied. She didn't really feel like talking right now. She looked straight ahead at the private box where Ann sat with her assistant. They were going over some papers and ignoring the row of expectant kids.

"You nervous?" Sheryl asked, waiting until Sam had passed by again. He had been circling impatiently, glancing at his watch, then at Ann.

"A little, I guess," Caroline said.

"Don't worry. If anyone is on the team, it'll be you."

"Keep it down!" Brad spat through clenched teeth, careful not to be heard by Sam. Sheryl glanced at him as if he were some kind of insect. His pal, Tom, who did everything Brad did, glared at her.

"Well at least we know who won't be picked," Sheryl said, looking back at Caroline, loud enough that both boys heard her. Caroline had kept quiet about her hopes of being chosen. She felt that it was just too much to expect in her first year of jumping. Part of her had a different attitude. That part of her knew how well she had done at various events over the summer. That part of her argued that her performance guaranteed her a spot on the Jump Alberta team.

"I don't know what scares me more," Sheryl said. "Being picked or not being picked. I know how my parents will react if I'm not."

"What's more important to you?" Caroline asked.

Sheryl looked at her, startled, and Caroline knew her words had come out more harshly than she had intended. She was nervous and a little tired of Sheryl's obsession with her parents' wishes. She wanted to tell her to do what she wanted, not what her parents wanted.

There was a sudden murmuring and the tension level shot up noticeably. Caroline turned back to see Ann and her assistant walk out of the booth, still deeply engrossed in paperwork. Maggie stood up straight and put the heavy silver bit and the polishing cloth on the rail beside her. Both items slipped unnoticed onto the dirt floor.

Ann walked up to the riders, wearing her usual jodhpurs and an expensive-looking high-collared shirt. She was only a few feet away from them when she finally looked up from the work she and her secretary had been going over. She turned to Sam, who waited patiently for her to speak. Caroline remembered the way she had seen Ann treat Sam over the summer and a thought occurred to her: Ann acted like she owned him.

"Well!" Ann said at last. "Don't we all look excited!"

She placed her hands on her hips and walked slowly along the line, looking to Caroline like a general inspecting the troops.

"I suppose you all know that Jump Alberta is fast approaching. As usual, Glennmohre will be fielding a team for the event. As you also know, for the past five years we have brought home the cup! I plan to make this the sixth year and, with that in mind, I have selected the members of my class who will represent Glennmohre Stables."

She stopped in the centre of the line and held out a hand casually. Her assistant handed her a folder. Caroline and Sheryl glanced at each other, eyes wide, visibly nervous. Ann opened the folder and paused dramatically to look over the list inside.

"I don't have to tell those who are picked what an honour it is to compete for our Stable. Likewise, those of you who did not make it know you are nevertheless a privileged few.

Whether you compete or not, we are still part of the same team."

Caroline glanced past her as something caught her eye. Maggie was standing at attention, her right hand up in a stiff salute. She mouthed each of Ann's well-rehearsed lines in perfect time with her. It was a speech she had obviously heard many times before. Caroline grinned at Maggie's antics, despite her tension.

Ann held up the list and looked at the riders. "I will call the names in alphabetical order." She paused one last time, and Caroline heard the creak of leather as everyone sat forward in the saddle.

"Anderson, Bradford," Ann called out. Brad sat up in his saddle, shocked and pleased, grinning madly. He cast a sarcastic glance at Sheryl, his response to her comment moments before.

"Chen, James."

"Danchuck, Thomas."

Tom turned to his friend Brad and they slapped each other on the arm. Both of them had made the team.

With each name called out, Caroline felt a strange thrill and a sense of disappointment. She wanted to hear her name and wondered why it wasn't called. She tried to tell herself this happened all the time. With a surname starting with an O, she was always one of the last to be called.

"Harrolds, Karen," Ann called out in her same tone. Caroline had another realization as she waited. Ann must have practised long and hard to perfect her public-speaking voice.

Caroline and Sheryl looked at each other, knowing that Innis, Sheryl was the next name in alphabetical order. Sheryl looked up at the high ceiling, as if praying. The sound of the rain pouring on it was even louder in the silent wait for Ann to call the next name.

"Kline, Michael," Ann called out. Caroline felt a sinking feeling in her stomach. She glanced at her friend, seeing how shaken she was by the news. Caroline reached out and grabbed her hand to comfort her and to help herself through the next few minutes.

"Nichols, Meghan," Ann said. There was a quickly silenced shriek as the girl realized she had made the team. Two more names had to be called for the eight-person team. Caroline clenched her fist on the reins, felt Sheryl grip her other hand even tighter. O was next. It had to be Owen!

"Owen, Caroline." There was an audible intake of breath from the students surrounding her. Caroline barely noticed.

"Stevenson, Brittany," Ann continued.

Caroline glanced over at Sheryl, mouth gaping, hardly able to believe what she had just heard. Sheryl was smiling now, looking genuinely pleased for her friend.

"Did you hear that too?" Caroline said at last. Sheryl was about to speak when Ann began again.

"Congratulations to the 1996 Glennmohre Stables team!" Ann called out. She nodded to Sam and he nudged his horse forward. In the tradition of the Stable, the team rode forward and did a kind of victory lap around the arena. Caroline realized she was still holding Sheryl's hand. She let it slowly slip away as she kneed Wallace forward. The other riders and the grooms, and even Ann, applauded them individually as they rounded the far end and came back to the main group. As Caroline passed Maggie, she lifted up her right hand and Caroline reached down to return the high-five. Maggie was laughing. Then, again following Sam's lead, the team whipped their helmets from their heads and threw them into the air, whooping at the top of their lungs.

"Don't forget, everyone!" Ann shouted loud enough for all the riders to hear. "This Friday is the annual Stable Barbecue. Everyone's invited, along with your families! We'll make the formal announcement then!"

"Are you okay?" Caroline asked Sheryl as she joined her once more. For the first time she noticed the others. Each one of them looked miserable, trying hard to mask disappointment for the sake of the ones who had been picked. Caroline could see that Sheryl was upset, despite her brave front.

Sheryl nodded. "I guess I wanted to be picked more than I realized. I'm just glad that you made it at least." She managed a smile, and Caroline felt a little guilty. She wasn't sure if she would feel as happy for her friend if the situation were reversed.

Ann had been congratulating the group of chosen riders, who had clustered together, talking excitedly amongst themselves. Caroline and Sheryl were between them and the rest of the class.

"Congratulations, Caroline," Ann said, coming over and raising her hand to shake. Caroline hesitated a second, not knowing if it was proper manners to dismount first. Ann had moved so quickly she had little choice but to shake hands still mounted.

"Thank you for picking me," Caroline replied.

"You more than proved yourself this summer."

"Wallace did pretty good, too," Caroline said, patting him on the neck. She had ridden him in every event since her first. He loved to jump and, ham that he was, he loved the adoration of the crowd.

"Actually," Ann said, looking Wallace over. "I meant to talk to you about that. Wallace is a fine pet, but I don't think he's quite up to the standards of Glennmohre Stables."

There was an awkward pause as Caroline assimilated this last statement.

"You don't want me to ride Wallace anymore?" Caroline said at last. Sheryl had been sitting still while Ann spoke to Caroline. Ann had completely ignored her.

"Maybe I should go," she said, "and get Stirling cleaned up."

Ann glanced at her quickly, as if noticing her for the first time, then looked back at Caroline.

"This is one of the best stables in North America. There are any number of fine horses for you to ride. Wouldn't it be exciting to ride a horse of exceptional breeding?"

Caroline felt Sheryl try to slip away unnoticed. She quickly reached out to grab her arm. She wanted to somehow include her in this.

"What about Stirling?" she blurted out. "Could I ride him?" Too late she realized that her suggestion might only make Sheryl feel more left out. The only reason she could ride Stirling in Jump Alberta was because Sheryl couldn't.

Ann once more looked at Sheryl, then at Stirling.

"Sheryl," she said, "didn't you want to clean Stirling?"

Knowing she was dismissed, Sheryl clucked softly and Stirling began to walk away. Caroline watched them go, feeling miserable for her friend. Ann waited until she was far enough away before continuing.

"Have you forgotten what happened at your first event riding Stirling?" Caroline shook her head. She could still clearly remember falling from him when he had suddenly spooked.

"Sheryl is your friend," Ann continued. "But we both know that she has never put her heart into jumping the way you and these others have."

"She tries her hardest," Caroline said, wanting to defend Sheryl.

Ann smiled faintly, as if humouring an infant.

"Of course she does. She doesn't take that extra step, that's all. The thing that separates a champion from the talented amateur is the ability to pick the right horse ... and the need to win. I think you should forget about Sheryl and Stirling and concentrate on what you have to do to become number one."

With that, she gave Wallace a pat and turned back to her assistant, who still hovered at her elbow holding files. Ann began to look over papers as she headed back out of the arena. Caroline watched her go, softly stroking Wallace's neck. After a few moments she urged him forward, to join Sheryl in the stables.

11

A Final Lesson

Y ou're doing great!" Sheryl shouted.

Caroline and Wallace rounded the next turn and sped up as they approached the jump. She felt the now-familiar lurch in the pit of her stomach as Wallace left the ground and soared gracefully over the exact centre of the jump. He landed well and she allowed him to canter around, keeping his movements supple and graceful. As usual, he pranced a little, knowing that he had done well.

"Good boy, Wallace!" Sheryl said as they trotted over to the fence. When Caroline had finished her work in the stables, she had decided to give Wallace a work-out, since he had been stuck in the paddock all day. Sheryl sat on the fence with Ian and Jimmy on either side of her like bookends. The four of them had been nearly inseparable in the weeks since Caroline's first event. The introduction of Sheryl into the little gang had been so smooth and easy that it seemed that she had always been part of it.

"He's amazing!" Sheryl said. "Too bad Ann won't let you ride him in Jump Alberta. You two are so good together." Sheryl patted Wallace's neck, and he seemed to bow in appreciation of the praise. Then Sheryl put her hand over her mouth, realizing what she had just blurted out.

"What's the matter?" Ian said, noticing Sheryl's reaction.

Caroline just looked over at Sheryl, who grinned and shrugged.

"You have to tell them eventually," she said. Caroline had been waiting for the right time to tell Ian and Jimmy that she was on the team. She slipped off Wallace and began to work on the cinch under his belly. She'd had enough riding today. Jimmy and Ian looked at each other.

"Is this girl stuff or something?" Ian asked mischievously.

"No, it's not girl stuff!" Caroline said, blushing. "I was picked for Jump Alberta."

Ian and Jimmy looked at her, then at each other. Ian started to laugh. Jimmy and Sheryl seemed puzzled at his reaction, as was Caroline.

"You're on the team?" Jimmy said. "That's good, right?"

"What's so funny, Calder?" Caroline finally asked.

Ian wiped his eyes; he was laughing so hard that tears flowed. "You start jumping, what, two months ago?" he said at last. "And you're on the team for the finals." He shook his head and smiled at her.

"Aren't you going to congratulate her?" Sheryl asked.

"Congratulations, Owen," Ian said. He still smiled at her, shaking his head at the turn of events.

"Congratulations," Jimmy added. "I always knew you'd make the team."

"You never even heard of the team two months ago!" Ian replied, ribbing him. "So, what will we do to celebrate?"

"First, let's get out of here." Caroline said, glancing at her watch. "We still have to feed and water our horses. And we'd better hurry if we want to get to Sheryl's pool while it's still hot out."

The three of them slid off the fence to join Caroline in the paddock. Caroline was the first to see Sam emerge from the stables, apparently looking around for someone.

"Caroline!" Sam shouted when he spotted her.

She sighed and looked at her friends, rolling her eyes.

"What does he want now?" Sheryl said. "You've finished for the day already!"

"I better go find out."

She walked over to him quickly, hoping to get the matter over with.

"I'm glad I caught you," he said as she stepped up to him. He looked as miserable as ever. "One of the grooms went home sick. I'd like you to fill in for her, just for a couple of hours."

"But I was just leaving. I've made plans with my friends."

Sam shrugged. "Plans change. I was planning on going home. Now Ann's asked me to stay longer to get these horses in shape for competition."

Caroline wanted to say no, but she knew that Sam would hold it against her for a very long time. She nodded.

"Good. Start in the east stable."

With that he turned around and strode off. Caroline sighed once more and walked back to her friends. She knew the look on her face showed that Sam hadn't given her good news. If she worked fast, maybe she could still join them later.

***

It was past seven when Caroline finally finished her work. The other grooms had told her to take shortcuts so she could leave earlier. Even her father had told her much the same when she had called to tell her parents what was going on. Not doing a thorough job cleaning the stalls would get her out sooner, but it wasn't fair to the horses.

Sore and tired, in need of a change of clothes and a long shower, Caroline walked to the indoor arena in search of Sam, to let him know she was done for the night.

She heard noises coming from inside. As she approached, she found the doors closed and a "Do Not Enter, Training" sign on them. She ignored the sign and went in. At the opposite end of the arena, Sam was riding Stirling, having him leap different styles of jumps, many much higher than anything Caroline had ever tried. She wasn't sure if Stirling had ever jumped anything that high before, either.

During the past two months, she had never been able to watch Sam train a horse. With her job at the Stables, she had often seen him at work, but had always been too busy to just stop and watch. Slipping into the shadows, she stood studying him, unobserved.

She had no idea how long the two of them had been practising, but by the sweat Stirling had worked up, she guessed it had been a long time.

Stirling seemed nervous at some of the jumps, yet Sam kept pushing him, forcing him to go on.

"Come on!" Sam yelled as Stirling shied away. It was a simple crossbar, but something had the horse spooked. It reminded her of the first time she had jumped Stirling in competition. Caroline could see Sam's frustration grow as Stirling kept refusing his commands.

"We're paid a lot of money to turn you into a champion! And I'll make you do it, one way or the other!" Sam slapped his riding crop; the loud crack made both Caroline and the horse start.

She could see Stirling was frightened now. His ears lay flat on his head and his nostrils flared. He was an unusually high-strung horse and he sensed Sam's growing anger. Sam twisted in the saddle, gripping the reins tightly, pulling the horse's head in the direction he wanted him to go. Caroline almost stepped out of her hiding spot, knowing Sam was hurting the horse's sensitive mouth. Even though he was using all his force and skill, he could barely keep the horse in check.

Finally, Stirling began to follow Sam's orders and started to jump again. Caroline sighed with relief. Now maybe Sam wouldn't be so hard on him.

They circled the end of the arena, then Sam turned Stirling in the direction of a jump at least five feet high. Stirling, although still nervous, seemed ready to take it. Then, once more, at the very last second, he slid to a complete halt. Sam came out of the saddle and for a moment Caroline thought he would fly over Stirling's head. Only his skill and sheer strength stopped him from crashing into the wooden bars.

"You stupid beast!" Sam shouted, his accent thickening with anger. He was absolutely furious, his cap flying off unnoticed as he began to slap Stirling with his crop.

She couldn't stand it. "Stop it!" she screamed, running out from her hiding spot. "Leave him alone!"

Startled to hear her voice behind him, Sam let his tight grip on the reins slacken. Stirling felt the release of pressure and knew it was his chance to escape. He bolted, galloping directly toward the far end of the arena.

She could only watch helplessly as Sam struggled to get the panicked horse back under control. They circled around the ring, once or twice slamming into the high fence that surrounded it.

Finally Sam managed to regain control. He walked Stirling around the arena, yanking cruelly on the reins. Caroline could see the bit dig into Stirling's mouth.

"What were you thinking?" Sam shouted as he rode slowly up to her. "You could've killed us both!"

It took a second for her to decipher his words. His heavy accent thickened when he was angry.

"You're blaming me?" she shouted back, angry herself. "You had him frightened to death already! Then you started to whip him!"

"Who's the trainer?" Sam replied. "Do you think I'd be here if I didn't know what I was doing?" They glared at each other.

"What's going on here?"

Caroline and Sam turned to watch Ann emerge from her private booth. There was only one way in or out of the booth, through the arena. Caroline realized that Ann must have been there the whole time.

"Did you see what happened?" Caroline demanded.

"Of course I did," Ann said. "Lovely performance. From all three of you."

Caroline, her mind a little muddled by anger, grew more confused by Ann's attitude. She didn't seem to care about what had just happened.

"Didn't you see what Sam did to Stirling?" Caroline said again, hoping for a more reassuring response.

"That horse could have damaged the Stable or itself," Ann replied coolly. "It could have been an expensive mess."

"Is that all you care about?" Caroline said. She couldn't believe that anyone who loved horses would be so unfeeling. "This horse is so scared, pretty soon no one will be able to go near him."

"The girl's right, Ann," Sam said at last. "We have to give up. The animal just isn't a jumper."

"I pay you for results, not opinions," Ann said. Sam's face darkened. Caroline saw that he wanted to say more, but he held back. Ann turned to face Caroline. "And you should be glad, young lady. We're getting this horse ready for you. It seems you'll get your wish to ride him after all."

Caroline was puzzled now. She was still too angry to think clearly. "I thought you didn't think Stirling was good enough."

"It's called compromise," Ann said, sighing. "Something all too necessary in the adult world. Sheryl's parents were upset to discover she hadn't made the team. I thought letting Stirling jump would take some of the edge off. They accepted, of course. After I explained that a good showing would increase Stirling's resale value immensely."

"But he's Sheryl's horse! They wouldn't sell him!"

Sam snorted and Ann looked at him knowingly.

"Get that animal put away and this place cleaned up," Ann ordered, heading back to her booth. "We'll keep what happened here to ourselves." Caroline felt her anger rising once again. Ann spoke to them as if they were slaves.

"Well, I won't keep it to myself! Neither Sheryl nor her parents will board Stirling here after I tell them what I saw. And neither will anyone else!"

This made Ann stop. She turned slowly to face Caroline. She was shocked to see that Ann's usual composure had been replaced by anger. The change was even more frightening than Sam's temper.

"Are you threatening me?" Ann said. Her voice was tight and controlled, but the anger spilled out. Caroline didn't know how to react or what to say.

"Do you really think anyone would believe a word you had to say?"

"But it's the truth!"

"The truth is what I say it is!" Ann replied. "Who is more credible? Me or some little girl from Millarville?"

"Ann," Sam said. "Leave the girl alone."

She ignored him and continued glaring at Caroline.

"I suggest you remember that you're part of a team here. We all stick together, no matter what. Unless you no longer want to be part of the team?"

Caroline shook her head, looking away from Ann.

"Ann! For God's sake, leave the girl alone. It was my mistake!"

"Yes, it was. Now make sure you clean up."

With that, Ann walked off. This time she didn't turn back.

"Why is she so mean all of a sudden?" Caroline asked Sam. Embarrassed, she found she was nearly in tears.

"All of a sudden?" Sam said, shaking his head. "There was nothing sudden about it. You've just seen the real Ann at last."

12

Apology Not Accepted

Caroline fidgeted nervously as she sat in the waiting room outside Ann's office. When she arrived that morning for work as usual, she still hadn't decided what to do. After last night, she didn't know if she could face Ann and Sam every day. She couldn't pretend that nothing had changed, that she hadn't finally seen what horses and people really meant to Ann. But she still wanted to compete in Jump Alberta.

As soon as she arrived in the morning, a groom told her that Ann wanted to see her in her office. Now she stared at the clock on the wall. It had been nearly half an hour since Ann's secretary had informed her that Caroline was here.

Finally the door opened and Ann stepped into the waiting area, holding a file full of official-looking papers. Caroline felt a sick lurch in her stomach at the sight of her, but Ann ignored her as she went over the papers with her secretary. Finally she finished and looked over at Caroline.

"Come inside, please," she said, as formal as ever.

She stepped back through the door of her office and Caroline followed, realizing it was the first time she had been in there. It was very large, with high ceilings and dark wood panels covering the walls. The wood was actually difficult to see, since almost every free inch was covered with awards and photographs. Most were of champion horses, though some were of Ann with people Caroline didn't recognize.

Ann walked around the huge antique desk that occupied most of the area in front of the windows and sat down.

"Close the door, please."

Caroline closed it gently and turned once more to face the older woman. There were two empty chairs at the desk, but she didn't know if she should sit.

"Come over here," Ann said. "I don't like to have to shout."

You did plenty of shouting last night, Caroline thought. She said nothing as she stepped toward the desk. Instead of speaking or inviting her to sit, Ann began looking over more papers. Caroline's initial nervousness was being replaced by irritation. She knew that Ann was ignoring her deliberately, trying to make her feel small.

"You wanted to see me," she said, fed up at last. Her voice didn't sound quite as forceful as she had hoped.

Ann glanced up from her papers and looked at her as if she had suddenly remembered she was there.

"In my day, children waited for their elders' permission to speak." Ann's voice was icy. Finally she closed her files.

"I suppose I should get to the point." Ann leaned forward, elbows on the desk, clasping her hands together. "I think we owe each other an apology after last night. I was a little cross with you. I was upset with Sam's handling of the horse. I shouldn't have taken it out on you and I apologize."

"It sounded like you made Sam treat Stirling that way."

Ann looked exasperated and waved her hand in the air.

"It doesn't matter what you heard!" Caroline watched as Ann fought to keep her temper under control. "I am not going to play some childish game of who said what. I have apologized for losing my temper and now I am waiting for you."

"You want me to apologize for losing my temper last night?" Caroline asked.

Ann sighed and leaned back in her chair, crossing her arms.

"I may have thought you a little unpolished, young lady. Until now I have never had reason to think of you as stupid."

Caroline felt her cheeks burn. She said nothing as she and Ann glared at each other from across the wide desk.

"All right," she said at last. "I apologize for losing my temper."

Ann continued to stare at her. "I was hoping for something a little more heart-felt, but I suppose that's all I should have expected." Ann shook her head slightly and opened her file. Caroline stood still, wondering if she was dismissed. At last she just turned and headed for the door.

"One more thing," Ann said. Caroline stopped and turned to face her again. "Perhaps I didn't make myself clear enough last night. If one word about Sam's handling of the horses gets out, I'll drop you from the team. And I'll make sure you never compete again."

***

"This is all very serious stuff," her father said, putting down his coffee. Caroline watched as he and her mother exchanged a worried glance.

"I don't see what's so serious!" Sheryl's father said. He had been pacing all evening, never once sitting down. Sheryl's mother was silent and looked extremely uncomfortable. She kept glancing at her watch. Ian and Jimmy hung around in the background with Sheryl. The boys had arrived earlier, since Sheryl had talked her parents into taking them all into Calgary with them. They were going to see a movie while her parents shopped. Caroline had been looking forward to not having to think for a few hours.

"Dad!" Sheryl said. "This is horrible! We can't let them keep mistreating horses! And I don't want to keep Stirling there any more!"

Her father looked at her as if she had just said something crazy. This meeting had come about rather suddenly. Sheryl's parents had driven up the moment Caroline had finished telling her own parents what had happened in Ann's office. Her father had asked them inside for coffee. He wanted to get their opinion, since they stabled their horse at Glennmohre. For Sheryl's sake, Caroline still hadn't mentioned that it was Stirling she had seen being beaten. She had to think of the best way to tell her and to make sure that Stirling was kept safe.

"It sounds serious to me," Caroline's mother said. "My daughter sees this man beating his animals. Then the owner, his boss, not only doesn't punish him, she threatens Caroline to keep quiet."

"Ann was just protecting her reputation. Who knows if Caroline saw what she thinks she saw. After all, these horses aren't pets. Sam has to discipline them," Sheryl's mother said.

"I think Caroline knows the difference between discipline and a beating," Caroline's father replied.

"I think we should be happy that she's on the team. And she said that Ann apologized for Sam's behaviour. Let's just leave it at that!" Sheryl's father said. He glanced at his own watch. It was obvious he was tired of the conversation.

"How would you feel if it was your horse he was beating?" Caroline's mother asked. Clearly she had also seen Sheryl's parents' annoyance. "And your daughter being threatened?"

"I think that this whole thing has been blown out of proportion. Glennmohre has a great reputation as a trainer of champion horses. And Ann is respected all over North America. She would hardly have to stoop to the kind of behaviour Caroline's describing."

Caroline realized that he was fooled by Ann's elegance and manners the same as everyone else. She knew that people usually saw only what they wanted to see in others.

"Caroline is a wonderful girl," he continued, "but perhaps she let her imagination run away with her."

"Caroline knows what she's talking about!" Ian blurted out. "Especially when it comes to horses!"

Everyone looked at him. He seemed embarrassed by his outburst. Caroline could see he was angry on her behalf. She was proud of him.

"Look at the time," Sheryl's father said. The others saw that he'd had enough. "We really have to get going." His wife stood quickly and buttoned her jacket as they both headed for the door. The kitchen was hot, but she had never bothered to take it off.

"Perhaps we can discuss this in a few days. When everyone can put a little perspective on it."

Sheryl's father looked at the kids, waiting for them to move.

"You guys better hurry if you still want us to drive you into town."

All four of them looked at each other. "No thanks, Dad," Sheryl said. "I think we'll just hang around here."

He looked a little surprised, then he shrugged. They left quickly, and the others sat in silence for a few moments. Sheryl held her head low and stared at her feet. Caroline guessed she was embarrassed by her parents' reaction.

"Well," Caroline's father said at last. "What now?"

"I think Caroline has a lot to consider," her mother said.

Caroline nodded. She was torn. She wanted to compete more than anything else. She knew that it was an important event for someone who wanted to continue jumping. But could she stay on a team run by people who beat their horses and cared only about money and appearances?

"I have to get some air," Caroline said at last. She walked down the hall and grabbed her jacket.

"You want some company?" Jimmy asked. She turned to see that Sheryl and Ian stood a little behind him, waiting. They all looked very concerned.

"Thanks," she said, "but I need to just think."

Caroline slipped on her old and faded jean jacket, stuffed her hands in the pockets and stepped outside. The sun was already touching the peaks of the mountains as she walked over to the paddock. Wallace was prancing around, chasing fireflies in the fading light. When he saw her he stopped his playing and loped over to her side.

"Hey, Wall," she said as he nudged her with his nose. She absent-mindedly stroked his neck and cheek. "What should I do, Wall?" He whinnied and nudged her once more, then spun around, ready to play again. When she didn't move, he stopped short and turned to face her, looking down at her questioningly. The thought of anyone treating Wallace the way she had seen Sam treat Stirling made her angry all over again.

As she watched Wallace trot playfully around the paddock, she realized that she had made up her mind. She couldn't be part of it any longer. Even if it meant she'd never have another chance to jump, she knew what she had to do.

"I'm quitting the team, Wallace."

13

Finding the Way

A tiny bubble of sap inside a log burst suddenly, sending sparks flying into the clear night. Caroline was startled and looked back at the fire, realizing that she had been daydreaming. She looked around at the others and saw that they were all lost in their thoughts, just as she had been.

Their horses were tied up nearby, and she could hear them shuffle their hooves as they nibbled at the low branches. The only other sounds were the distant chirp of crickets and the crackle of the fire. Caroline shivered a little and shifted closer to the fire. It was the end of August, and as soon as the sun dipped behind the mountains, the temperature dropped noticeably.

Like all of them, Ian leaned back, using his saddle as a support, his long legs sticking straight out in front, the sole of one boot occasionally licked by the flames. He didn't seem to notice as he tilted his head back and stared at the cloudless night sky.

Sheryl stared into the fire, the embers reflecting in her blue eyes, her arms wrapped tightly around herself. She rocked slightly back and forth and Caroline wondered what she was thinking.

She knew what Jimmy was thinking, the same thing he always did when they stayed after dark in the mountains. He looked fairly calm most of the time, but she knew any unexpected sound would startle him.

Another bubble of sap burst in the log and Jimmy, who had been looking into the woods, jumped. The look in his eyes was pretty funny.

"It's okay, Jimmy," Caroline said. "It's just the log."

"Yeah," Ian said, still gazing up at the stars. "A grizzly makes a lot more noise than that."

Caroline and Ian grinned at each other. Jimmy looked sheepish.

"Quit bugging him, you guys," Sheryl said. "He's not the only one who worries about bears."

"See!" Jimmy said. Caroline smiled. Jimmy had come a long way since first moving out here. But in some ways he was still a city kid. Of course, she'd never admit it to anyone, but she'd been known to get a little bear-spooked herself.

Right now, though, she had more important things on her mind.

"Must be nice," Jimmy said. "Finally getting a whole weekend off from the Stable."

"Yeah," Ian said. "Too bad it's the last weekend before school."

Jimmy and Sheryl groaned in unison. "Thanks for reminding me, Calder," Sheryl said. Caroline grinned. Even Sheryl was calling Ian exclusively by his last name.

"I'm going to have a lot more days off from Glennmohre," Caroline said, glad that the perfect opportunity had presented itself.

"How come?" Sheryl asked. They looked at each other from across the fire, and Caroline knew that her friend had already guessed why.

"Because I quit the team yesterday."

"You did?" Ian said. He and Jimmy were both sitting up straight now. They acted as if the news was a total shock to them, even after the discussion they'd all had two nights ago in her parents' kitchen.

"Good for you!" Sheryl said. She grinned at Caroline, looking proud of her.

"What did Ann say when you told her?"

Caroline laughed now, even though she hadn't been able to at the time. "Let's just say that if I used some of the words Ann did, I'd still be tasting soap."

They all laughed and looked at each other, as if unsure of how to react to the news.

"What about Jump Alberta?" Jimmy asked. "Does this mean you're not in it? After all that's happened?"

Caroline shrugged. It was the one part of her decision that still hurt.

"I guess not. Now that I'm not part of a team."

"That's just lousy," Ian said. His grin had disappeared.

"Why can't you still enter?" Jimmy asked.

Caroline felt tired suddenly. She hadn't expected this kind of questioning. She was glad she had told them; now she just wanted to move on.

"It's not that easy," Sheryl said when Caroline hesitated. "You need the right tack and clothes and stuff. And the entry fees are pretty expensive."

"So?" Ian replied. "We could probably borrow the tack. And I bet we could find a way to get the money together."

"How? I'm the only one who had a job this summer," Caroline said. She didn't have to remind anyone that it hadn't paid a cent. "And we have less than a month now."

"There's got to be a way," Jimmy said, almost to himself. Caroline saw that he had finally stopped worrying about bears.

"It's not just that," Sheryl added. "You have to be on a team, part of a Stable. You can't just enter on your own."

Ian and Jimmy looked at each other. They appeared determined to get Caroline into the competition, one way or another.

"Who says?" Ian said at last.

"Yeah," Jimmy added quickly. "Do you know for sure?"

Caroline looked at Sheryl. She had never thought about it before. "As far as I know," Sheryl said, thinking it over carefully. "There isn't a real rule or anything. But I'm pretty sure you have to represent a Stable. You can't just go in on your own."

"There's got to be a way to do it," Ian said. Caroline looked into the glowing embers of the fire and part of her wished he was right. Despite her wishing, she knew that it was nearly impossible.

"Even if we could do it," Sheryl said, "wouldn't it feel weird? Competing against your own team?"

"It happens all the time to pros," Jimmy said. "One week you're playing for Montreal, then boom! You're traded! The next week you're in Boston!"

Caroline could hardly compare her situation to professional hockey, but she knew that Jimmy had a point. "It would feel weird, I guess," she said. Actually, it would have bothered her only if Sheryl had been on the team.

"I don't know," Ian said, a sly grin on his face. "Going up against Ann's team? All those kids you used to train with? How would that make you feel, Owen?"

Caroline was grinning too. He knew her too well.

"Like kicking their butts!"

14

Millarville's Own

Why are you moping around?" Caroline's father asked. She looked over at him as he walked up, then turned away again. Wallace had been fed his evening meal and now stood near the shed, nearly motionless. She had been sitting on the fence, hands in the pockets of her jacket, just staring out across the fields. Try as hard as she could to think of other things, all that kept coming to mind was the fact that Jump Alberta was a week away and she wasn't in it. She had thought that she could move on, that she could forget about the whole thing. But as the actual day approached, it began to bother her more and more.

"Why don't we go for a ride into town?" he said, slipping his arm over her shoulder.

"I don't really feel like it," she said as politely as she could. She just wanted to be left alone. Even Wallace sensed it and was keeping his distance.

"Come on," he said. "Humour the old man, okay?" She tried to ignore him, but he kept insisting, and she realized that he wasn't giving up. She shrugged and slipped off the fence. Why not, she thought. It beats sitting here feeling sorry for myself.

Her father kept chatting away about nothing as his old pick-up jostled its way down the dirt roads. Caroline nodded politely when she had to and stared out the window. For the hundredth time, she thought about whether she had made the right decision in quitting the team. She had debated the same thing over and over for nearly three weeks.

Part of her depression was due to the fact that she had seen very little of her best friends lately. It seemed as if they were avoiding her. They were always busy doing something and every time she asked what, they gave her a different excuse.

School had started again and she found it had actually helped, giving her other things to think of.

Some of the time.

It would have been better if Sheryl at least went to the same school. Caroline looked up, jolted from her thoughts when she noticed that the jostling had stopped and her father had parked his truck outside his auction house. She looked around at the parking area at the side and thought there were a lot of cars. It was a Saturday and her father rarely held an auction on a Saturday evening.

"I thought we were going into town," Caroline said when her father asked her to follow him.

"I just wanted to show you something first."

He walked quickly ahead of her and opened the front door of the building, waving her in. She heard the loud hum of voices as soon as she stepped inside and she found herself curious as to what was going on in there.

"Surprise!" dozens of voices called out as she stepped into the auditorium. Caroline felt her cheeks flush as she saw all the people standing there cheering her. Her best friends stood in the centre with her mother, grinning wider than anyone else. She looked up at her father, completely puzzled.

"Look at the sign!" her mother said as she rushed out of the crowd to hug her. Caroline looked up at the podium where her dad stood on auction nights. There was a huge canvas sign hung above it that read: "Millarville Supports Its Entry in Jump Alberta: Caroline Owen!"

She looked at her parents, still bewildered. "I still don't get it!"

"Just wait," her mother said.

As she watched, she saw old Mr. Calhoun walk over to the podium to test the mike. He wore the same silly cowboy shirt and huge hat he wore at every gymkhana.

"Well, folks! It looks like our guest of honour is here and we better get this show on the road."

There was a little more applause and some laughter.

"I'd like to first introduce the masterminds of this little surprise party," he said and held his hand over his eyes, peering theatrically into the crowd. "Come on up here!"

There was more applause and Caroline laughed in delight as Sheryl, Ian and Jimmy were dragged up on the stage beside him. Ian held a large brown envelope, nervously passing it from one hand to the other. She saw that the shelves and pens that her father used to display the items up for auction were full. Home-baked pies, jars of preserves and all kinds of handmade crafts packed the shelves. She saw manufactured items like bikes and chainsaws, even a small riding mower. Each item had a card attached to it, identifying the person or business who had donated it.

"All of us have seen a lot of these three kids in the last week or so, haven't we?" There was more applause, and the three seemed to look even more nervous, trying to hide behind each other.

"They've been busy gathering together all kinds of wonderful stuff to raise money for a worthwhile cause! To get Millarville entered for the first time in Jump Alberta!" He paused as the crowd applauded and cheered loudly. "And now let's present the girl who's going to bring the trophy home next Saturday! Caroline Owen!"

There was more applause and Caroline was led to the podium by her parents. She stood in the centre, surrounded by her friends and family.

"Caroline," Mr. Calhoun began. He took the mike from its stand and crouched down beside her, placing a huge calloused hand on her shoulder. His shirt smelled faintly of mothballs. "I want you to know that the people of your community have banded together to make sure you do us proud in next week's competition.

"A lot of fine people have donated their time as well as a few more…tangible things," he grinned at the audience as he said the last words, "which we're going to auction off tonight to help pay the way for Caroline. We want her to look her best when she represents our town in Jump Alberta." There was more applause and he stood up once again facing the crowd. "So before you all get tired of listening to my voice, let me turn the mike over to Caroline's dad and the owner of Owen's Own Auction House. Mr. John Owen."

There was more applause as Caroline's father strode up to the podium, smiling broadly. He grinned at the crowd, and Caroline was impressed by how cool her father seemed up there, how comfortable he was in front of so many people.

"Usually as the auctioneer, I let someone else do the bidding," he said, taking the microphone. "But I have to tell you, I've been eyeing Helen Carson's bumbleberry pies and I mean to take them home myself! So let's start!"

She saw that her father had a very similar style to Mr. Calhoun, but he seemed more natural to her, less of a ham. Caroline applauded along with the others, then she and her mother waded through the crowd to the rear of the auditorium, while people congratulated her and wished her luck. Caroline could only smile back and nod occasionally. She felt overwhelmed by it all. Sheryl, Ian and Jimmy also managed to thread through the crowd toward her.

"Now I know where you guys have been the last couple of weeks," Caroline said as they stood around her. They all shrugged and grinned. Now that it was all actually happening, they seemed a bit dazed as well.

"Your dad sounds amazing," Sheryl said. They stopped to listen to him calling out the bids, pointing to various people as he did. "I've never been to a real auction before."

Caroline agreed. He was pretty amazing.

"We also have something else to give you," Ian said. He handed her the large manila envelope she had seen him holding on the stage.

"What is it?" she asked, taking it from him.

"Open it and see," Jimmy said. Grinning at them, she lifted the flap and looked. She saw an official-looking document inside. A little shakily, Caroline pulled it out and read it carefully. Even then she still wasn't sure if it was really what she thought it was.

"It's real!" Sheryl said. "That's your official entry to Jump Alberta! You're all signed up!"

Caroline was speechless. Instead of trying to think of something to say, she threw her arms around Sheryl.

"Thank you!" she said a last.

She saw Jimmy and Ian look at her, keeping their distance a little.

"Come on," Sheryl said. "Give her a hug. She won't bite."

She hugged them both, a little more awkwardly than she had Sheryl. The four of them stood around in silence; all of them had the same silly expression on their faces. They just listened to the sound of her dad calling out the bids. The words and rhythm flowed so fast, it sounded as if he were speaking some foreign language.

Sheryl suddenly took Caroline's hand, as if remembering something.

"Will you guys excuse us for a minute?"

Without waiting for an answer, Sheryl dragged Caroline around the edges of the crowd toward a small door in the very back of the building. Inside was a small storage area and her father's office. It was crowded with junk and her father's files. The room had looked very much the same for as long as she could remember, but in the middle of the floor was something new. A metal box about three feet high and four feet wide sat apart from the clutter. Caroline recognized it immediately.

"That's your tack box," she said to Sheryl.

"Not any more," Sheryl replied, grinning. "It's my present to you."

Caroline walked over to it, running her hand along the surface.

"I can't take this. What will you use?"

Sheryl shrugged. "I wouldn't worry about that. It's empty, anyway. My parents would have a fit if I gave you my tack, too. But I don't think we'll have any trouble filling it after tonight."

Sheryl was still grinning as she reached behind a full-length antique mirror. She pulled out a grey garment bag.

"I brought you one more thing."

She handed the garment bag to Caroline, who again recognized it immediately.

"I *know* I can't take this," she said.

"Sure you can. I won't need it any more."

"Why not?"

Sheryl shrugged and sat down on the lid of the tack box.

"Because I quit the class too."

Caroline wasn't really surprised by the news. She knew that Sheryl had never been as involved in jumping as she had.

"What did your parents say?"

"What do you think?" Sheryl paused. "They'll get over it. With my luck they've already signed me up at some ski school!"

Sheryl stood up and hung the bag on a hanger, unzipping it.

"Go on, try it on," she said.

A few minutes later, Caroline turned around to look at herself in the antique mirror. Sheryl had used a rag to wipe off the weeks of dust it had collected sitting in the storage area. Caroline hardly recognized the young girl who stared back. The green riding coat and sparkling white breeches had been custom-tailored for Sheryl, but they fit Caroline perfectly. She adjusted the brim of her helmet.

"Wow," Sheryl said, looking at her friend. "You look like a winner."

Caroline looked at herself again. Whatever happened next week, she did feel like a winner already. She hugged Sheryl once more. "Thanks," she said. "For everything."

"No problem," Sheryl said. "That's what friends are for."

***

It was past ten when the bidding was finally over. Mr. Calhoun once more climbed the stairs to the podium to thank everyone for their participation. Caroline and the others were called back on stage. Sheryl had wanted her to keep wearing the riding outfit, to show it off to the crowd, but Caroline had refused. She was glad she had changed back to her regular clothes as she looked out over the sea of faces.

"Caroline," Mr. Calhoun said. It took her a few seconds to realize he was looking at her, holding out the microphone. There was applause and he thrust the microphone in front of her, asking her to say a few words.

"I...I...don't know what to say," she stammered. She had never had to speak in front of this many people before. "I guess...thank you."

There was more applause, then Caroline was hugged by everyone around her until they all became a blur.

"Now!" Mr. Calhoun called out. "Let's all have some fun." Someone had set up a huge stereo system on a table in the corner. Loud country music began to play from the sound system and people started to break into groups. Caroline stood facing her friends, who were now grinning at her, looking relieved to be out of the spotlight.

"You guys are too much!" she said at last, trying to hug them all at the same time. "I don't know how I'll ever thank you for this."

"You just have to win next week," Ian replied. She smiled at him. They all stood on the sideline while the older people began to dance. They were shouting to be heard over the music.

"Is that all?" she said. They all knew that the level of competition would be the highest yet. It would also mean that she would be seen by some of the most important people in jumping. She only hoped that she and Wallace could pull it off. She usually competed for herself; now she had the entire town relying on her.

"Don't worry," Sheryl said, as if reading her mind. "If anyone can do it, you and Wall can."

They stopped trying to shout over the music and just watched the dancers for a while. A group of about twenty people had formed three lines in the centre of the floor, doing a dance called the Cowboy Cha Cha, all in perfect unison.

"How do they do that?" Jimmy asked, watching them move together.

"Practice," Caroline's father said. He and Caroline's mom had two-stepped up to the kids. Both of them were grinning, their cheeks flushed from dancing and the rising heat in the hall. All her life, Caroline had seen her parents dance, usually a slow one on the back porch as the sun went down. It was the first time she had seen them dance in public.

"You keep standing around like that, you'll grow roots," her mother said. "Come on up!"

The four of them looked at each other. They hadn't thought of dancing until that second.

"You wanna try?" Jimmy asked. He had a weird lopsided grin on his face.

"Dancing?" Caroline replied. "I don't know. I've never tried it."

"Come on," Ian said. "Compared to jumping a horse over fences, how hard can it be?"

"Since when are you an expert on it, Calder?" she shot back.

To her surprise, he and Sheryl blushed.

"I've been kind of teaching him," Sheryl said, her cheeks glowing. Caroline grinned at her two friends. She thought it was time that she and her only girlfriend discussed a few things. She saw Ian and Jimmy waiting expectantly. Maybe Ian was right. Compared to show jumping, how difficult could it be?

"Let's give it a try," she said. The four of them walked bravely into the pounding music and the crowd of dancers.